NEVER FAR

Jamie Brookes

ISBN-13: 9798879594072

Independently published

Cover design by: Nafeesa J
Printed in the United Kingdom

CONTENTS

CHAPTER 1

Voices from the Kitchen

When recounting this type of memory, films depict a person staring into a balled-up, tear-soaked tissue while they whimper specifics like "It was a Tuesday... it had just gone nine in the morning." I don't recall such details.

I know it was 7th January, I know it was 1991 because I was five years old and little mattered more than my 25-metre swimming badge and the emerging phenomenon of the Teenage Mutant Ninja Turtles. But I don't know the day of the week and I don't remember what time it was when I was first told. In later life, I've learned this was a coping mechanism from shock, but the main thing I remember from 7th January is the voices from the kitchen.

My memories have taken on a discoloured, almost dirty sheen. Like a 1970s B-movie, the pastel tones are different shades of brown and cream. Some of the more distinct memories come in the form of tastes and most potently in sounds and smells. Like many people, my Nana Beatrice liked the smell of a struck match. The coarse, festive scent of flint and burning wood always brought a satisfied wiggle to her nose and brow. But it is the exact opposite for me. Bad weather had damaged the generator on the west side of Heaval summit in Castlebay that day and much of the village's power was cut, which led to the houses being lit by candlelight. Throughout the sickening evening, while being chaperoned from house to house, room to room, all I could smell was that flint spark as matches were struck to maintain light.

The hushed tones everyone used that day were perhaps the most unsettling thing for a child of my age. Everyone's face was so gravely serious; conversation volume was lowered to an adult level where children could only detect faint murmurs; eyes would flicker nervously and doors were pulled slowly shut when anyone realised I was in earshot.

There are few things as painful to hear as a human sliding helplessly towards tears while their staccato, stabbing sentences desperately claw for composure. You're urging them to survive it but a torrent of wailing emotion thunders forth and won't be stopped. I heard that sound countless times that afternoon. People being swept into an ocean of grief while trying to remain as quiet as possible. It's most disturbing when you begin to recognise the voices that are in such despair. One by one I deciphered Nana, Mum and Glenda from next door slipping off that cliff into endless tears punctuated by sharp gasps.

"Good evening and welcome to the BBC News at eight o'clock. A small town on the Isle of Barra in the Outer Hebrides has been cast into the world media's spotlight after a tragedy at a local school."

I was to "stay in the dining room whilst the adults talk", my Grandpa exclaimed whenever I attempted to inch the door open and investigate the nameless cloud which had fallen over our house. I felt alone, but calm.

The grandfather clock that stood in the corner next to the window watching over the room had never kept accurate time, which made me feel a little detached and disorientated as the light faded. I was surrounded by potential sources of light, like the garish table lamp that my mother had brought from a car boot sale in Badabrie or the standard lamp in the corner with a thick fabric shade that was clearly a charity offering from Nana years ago. But I did not use any of them. I sat at the dining table and waited to be summoned while the drizzly early evening became nighttime.

Outside I heard the crunch of gravel underfoot as footsteps made their way up our garden path towards the house. The toxic aura of that day had clearly begun to disturb me because this banal, everyday sound of footsteps brought a feeling of total vulnerability. My mind was running riot, conjuring images of who could be approaching.

I exhaled slowly as I watched my Aunty Gill come into view outside. She was heading for the 'family entrance' to our house, on the right-hand side where you can go straight into the kitchen. She was clearly distressed as I watched her profile shuffle past the window fiddling with her keys. Aunty Gill was a prison officer, a sturdy and forthright middle-aged woman who was seldom warm but always loving, and hugely wise. She moved closer to the house tentatively as if shuffling her words, preparing sentences. She stopped and slowly put her forehead between her swollen thumb and index finger, massaging her temples while her eyes seemed to let go of her surroundings and wander to a place that was less daunting.

It was at this point that her gaze wandered through the window and fell on me, her nephew, sitting alone in the dark. Startled, she screamed. My hands gripped the chair beneath my legs at the piercing sound. I heard the kitchen door bang against the cupboard unit as Aunty Gill bounded in and enquired loudly, "Why is he just sitting in the dark!?" I listened as my aunty toured the room doling out affection to the needy and beginning to take her own first steps on that slippery slope towards tears that I'd been listening to for hours.

It was at this point that the chatter seemed to pick up as the occupants of the kitchen gave Aunty Gill some kind of update. I knelt down and positioned my ear next to the cold sliver of air flowing through the keyhole and the voices immediately gained clarity and volume.

"I know, Mum, I know," she said to Nana, "but please stop crying. We need to just... we need to... Dad, sort her out, will you? We need to be strong right now." Big Aunty Gill had only been in the house 30 seconds and was already taking the lead. There was shuffling, and chair legs whined as they were dragged across the tiled floor around the kitchen table. I listened and began assigning the voices to bodies, building a picture of the group in the kitchen. Gill was counselling, Grandpa, ever the traditional strong silent type, was offering episodic comfort to Nana but I couldn't make out the lower tones chattering seriously in the deep background. Mum and Glenda, I suspected, debating the nameless incident over their mugs of sugary tea.

My back strained with the tension of hunching towards the keyhole but I persevered. The oddest and most frustrating behaviour was the radio being switched on and off. At that young age I attributed this to the power outage, but in hindsight it was a battle between those in the kitchen who wanted information and those who could not bear it.

"From the headquarters of ITN, the *News at Ten* with Trevor McDonald," crackled the TV from the distant living room. "Good evening. Deaths have been confirmed as Castlebay's nightmare continues. We have an extended edition of tonight's programme as we report on what is being called Scotland's Darkest Day."

Rain fell softly, spitting along the dining room window, and I began to feel the cold. Still filled with a mixture of respect for and fear of my grandpa I peeled the door open and gently aimed my voice towards the half-open kitchen door.

"I'm really cold, can I come in?"

The voices fell silent and chair legs screeched against the floor with greater urgency. "Oh Christ, I'm sorry you've had to sit in there, lovey," said Aunty Gill, lunging from her seat to place an oversized, paw-like hand on my shoulder. Her arm curled round and ushered me into the room that I'd been mentally analysing for the best part of two hours. The kitchen's lemon colour scheme blinded me as the door was opened and I tentatively walked in. I scanned the room and saw that many of my deductions had been accurate. Grandpa leant awkwardly against the Rangemaster oven with his back to me and a hand on his hip. Nana was sitting in a chair, immaculately dressed but drenched in tears as she forced a smile at me from behind her china teacup. Our neighbour Glenda stood with a hand on her hip and the other dug into her hair in a classic pose of despair. It was at that point that I realised the low female mutter I'd thought was Mum talking to Glenda was actually a female police officer.

Mum was not there.

In the days that followed what would become known simply as 'Classroom B' back on 7th January 1991, everyone seemed to be busy, as if dressing an enormous room for a big event, running around, taking phone calls, rubbing furrowed brows. Everyone knew their job. Everyone but me.

Nana and Grandpa had all but moved in and Aunty Gill was preparing my dinner every evening. It was quite surreal. Figures of authority maintaining a familiar routine can create unparalleled levels of irrational acceptance in a child. The mere fact that Nana, Grandpa and Aunty Gill were apparently well versed in what needed to be done offered me some comfort and meant I wasn't immediately concerned as to the whereabouts of Mum. I was simply curious. In retrospect, this is a testament to my family's superhuman effort at maintaining normality in the house during that time.

I observed the patterns of life that my family were displaying and noted that, like superheroes and their alter-egos, I never saw everyone in the cottage at the same time. They were pulling shifts to look after me, which meant it was through necessity rather than choice. This was when I began to allow the dark clouds of doubt to waft into my subconscious.

CHAPTER 2

The Caledonian Sleeper

I suppose a flood of childhood memories is to be expected given the destination of my train today. It's a balmy London evening in July 2021 and I'm about to board the Caledonian Sleeper train.

It's a long trip but that's fine as I have a lot to tell you. I'm feeling good, full-bodied, almost complete. I think this trip is the right move. I've chewed it over for many years and have decided now, at the age of 35, is the time.

I've just arrived at Platform 1 on the far right-hand side of the dank, industrial bunker of London's Euston Station. Unlike the others that cater to the panting 'trundle trains' for local commuters or the humming, modern intercity engines, Platform 1 is reserved for the enchanting sleeper train, which nuzzles its way from London to some of the northernmost cities at the top of the British Isles in Scotland. I'm rather excited as I've heard much about this antiquated mode of transport but I've never experienced it. That changes this evening.

Leaving the shops and lights behind, the long concrete ramp leads me down to the platform, and the smell of overpriced pastries and coffee fades into the distance. At the far end of the station, the orange evening sun is oozing through promisingly.

"Coffee or tea, lovely?" a soft voice chirps from over my right shoulder as I walk down onto the platform, jolting me from my reverie. As I turn around I realise the meek voice belongs to a striking woman. A gentle but haunting Gaelic song of long flutes and rhythmic violins floats into the station building as my eyes rapidly study her – wild, glossy black hair, a cute face with almost childlike features. My heart throbs with heat and I struggle to cloak this from her. She's dressed in a Caledonian Sleeper uniform but her name badge is blank.

"Me?" I ask confusedly, struck by her stirring, almost fierce blue eyes which don't seem to fit with her timid voice. The flutes and violins have ceased and for a moment I'm unsure whether they came from the speaker system in the ceiling or my head. "I'm taking orders, lovely; depending on which carriage you're in your brew will reach you by Milton Keynes or Carlisle." The corners of her thin Celtic lips curl with playfulness. Her Scottish

JAMIE BROOKES

accent is so thick that her words must have to contort themselves around it. She immediately brings back memories of home.

"I'll have tea, Earl Grey, no milk, cabin 23, thank you," I reply excitedly as my mind paints the platform black and white, pumps imaginary billowing steam from the train and Laura and Alec from the 1940s classic *Brief Encounter* embrace on the step of a carriage to the sound of theatrical violins. What an absolute treat this journey is going to be.

I reach up and pull on the golden door handle, leaning backwards to lever it open, something which gives me great pleasure. Stepping on board, the chilly air of the station changes to a stuffy warmth redolent of the 1930s that crowds my nose, neck and ears. I'm immediately spellbound by the cinematic feeling of the carriage, the bijou, anachronistic cabins transport me to a time I've only seen on screen, when train travel was about privacy, cosiness and indulgent carriage decor. The whole thing is dedicated to the now outdated priorities of comfort and homeliness, with touches that would be deemed unnecessary on modern trains; miniature lampshades with those frilly tassels around the rim, tiny individual footmats by the door of each and every cabin. Bloody wonderful. There's a musty, used scent which may turn the noses of some first-time sleepers but for me it just adds to the feeling that I'm stepping backwards in time. Escaping.

Walking down the carriage's narrow corridor I slip past other passengers matching their tickets to the cabin numbers sitting in wooden frames on the wall. Two parents help their young adolescent sons into their compartment like the Railway Children fleeing London during the war for the safety of the countryside.

I hear the screaming hoot of the steam engine before smiling to myself bashfully; this is not a steam train, but an electric locomotive.

Tearful mothers wipe their cheeks with handkerchiefs from the platform, braced by their husbands while passengers hang from the windows waving goodbye with their caps. A large, rotund man in a cream suit struggles to lift his heavy cello aboard.

Mine is to be a short stay and so I don't have a large suitcase with me, just a modest overnight bag, which I'm glad of when I reach my charming but cramped cabin, number 23. It is approximately five feet square and my six foot one height lightly brushes the ceiling. I'm slightly underwhelmed to see that it is fabricated from what looks to me like the same materials as aeroplane toilet doors – plastic panels which seem to bend if you lean on them – but I don't mind as these things suggest I may be able to overhear my neighbours, a voyeuristic vice which I've always enjoyed. You discover the most meaningful things when studying those who are unaware.

The panels are coloured a saddle-brown colour in

a vain attempt to trick a passenger into thinking they are in fact wood. Standing at the door, there is a bunk on the right accessed via a metal ladder beneath which is a small armchair, side table and lamp which seemed to have been designed for the Borrowers rather than an actual human-sized human. Opposite this, on my left there is a small basin and mirror and directly facing me is the window, the top of which features a sliding slat to bring in the air... or disperse the musk. Many may think this cabin is terrible, but I think it's marvellous.

A speaker mounted in a 'walnut' wood box crackles to life.

"Good evening and welcome on board the Caledonian Sleeper to Fort William. For those not travelling with us tonight please disembark as the train will be leaving soon. Thank you." A catering worker rushes past my door with a trolley leaving the smell of roast chicken, steak and vegetables in his wake. No dry, bland, pre-packaged sandwiches aboard this service, just proper cooked food.

It's very film noir, I think to myself, the way the summer afternoon sun is cutting through the slats on the blind across my cabin window, painting slim shadows across the room and making everything appear to be behind some sort of grille. Yes, this current moment in my life feels very *Double Indemnity* as delicate jazz notes dance across piano keys. The silhouette of a slender man in a Panama hat pauses at the frosted glass window on the door to my cabin, takes a puff from a cigar, and then walks on.

Likening everything I see, hear or feel to a film is something that I have done for as long as I can remember. For some reason the movies I have seen are coded into my mind, forming a vast reference library, and I frequently stumble into scenes throughout my day, muttering to myself about my life's *mise en scène*. Years ago I wondered whether there was any specific use for this innate ability, if you can even call it an ability, but my research quickly revealed that the likes of Mensa would not be banging down the door to recruit me. It's just a quirk, a weird one and a useless one, and it can surface at unusual times. Whether I'm supposed to be feeling happy or upset, my mind will undoubtedly serve up a vase from a Hitchcock classic, how someone ordered coffee in a Tarantino scene or the way rain moved sadly across a window in a von Trier shot.

Today, I'm going home to Scotland. Somewhere I have neither wanted to go or been permitted to go since I left twenty years ago at the age of sixteen. You'd think my stomach would be a greenhouse of butterflies and my hands anxiously drumming on my knee but I feel quite calm. Maybe it's the thirteen-hour journey I know that separates me from my homeland and the nerves are reserving themselves for when I'm closer.

There's no movie reference for what happened up there, or for what is to come.

CHAPTER 3

Clay

As I unpack and arrange a toothbrush and paste, antiperspirant and some chestnut hair dye around the hilariously small vanity sink area, I hear a French voice wandering past the door, clearly engaged in a last-minute business call. She passes the frosted glass in my cabin door quickly but her deep Gallic drawl lingers, reminding me of the enchanting opening sequence to the French film Amélie. The characters are introduced via short but wonderfully intimate and revealing characteristics. Their name, a single like and a single dislike are all we're given as a viewer. "This is Joseph, he likes to pop the bubbles on plastic wrapping... this is Amandine, she doesn't like her fingers getting wrinkled in hot water... this is Suzanne, she likes sportsmen who cry with disappointment..." I am hugely interested in discovering the gritty, meaningful parts of a person; these honest and unique features are often the most fascinating.

With this in mind, I would say my own introduction would go something like: "This is Clay. Clay likes the sound of sharp-heeled brogues on cobbled streets and dislikes people who are unaware of their loud guffaws."

No, how about: "This is Clay. Clay likes lemon ice tea but only from a glass bottle and dislikes whisky, despite being a Scotsman."

No, OK, better one: "This is Clay. Clay likes the whining crow of seabirds and dislikes the heavy throb which rises in your chest when you're being chased."

I am infinitely intrigued by the granular detail of individual humans, it's so much more interesting, or, as Robin Williams' warm and wise character put it in *Good Will Hunting*, "All our little imperfections, that's the *good stuff*."

I think I'm especially in tune with such idiosyncratic traits because for most of my adult life I have had to cloak mine from those who I meet. I'm not permitted to show them the real man, whose real name is not Clay, whose real name has changed seven times so far. And whenever someone has gotten too close to my real likes or dislikes, my real imperfections, I've had to run. In the movies this is where my character would dramatically whisper, "I've had to run for so long, I don't know who I am any more," but I know precisely who I am. And by the end of this journey, you will too.

The train releases a deafening shriek of its whistle and slowly rocks into motion.

CHAPTER 4

A Watcher

The traffic is building up as the sleeper train slowly weaves its way from Euston up above the roads and gains speed in the evening rush hour. I'm taking solace in the fact that there isn't the relentless soundtrack of screaming sirens like where I live in London. The slim window slat is supplying an evolving story of smells: soupy engine fumes bleed into sharp kebab shop spice before mellowing into a malty brewery stench then finally something resembling normal air.

A glance at my Omega Seamaster shows it's only been a few moments since I left the station. Time is dragging. There was no need to tell you the brand of my timepiece just then, I could have just said "timepiece"; and while we're on the topic, I'm disappointed to hear myself use the term timepiece, when watch would have more than sufficed. Growing up there was a term for gentlemen who referred to their watch as their "timepiece", they were called "wankers," and somehow I have inadvertently become one. This is my first timepiece, because as a young boy I wore a Teenage Mutant Ninja Turtles watch which I'm not sure can be termed a timepiece. Such pretensions are not common in my vocabulary. I feel I am a grounded person deep down, but phrases like that seem to have found their way into me after moving to London eight years ago, perhaps as a way of trying to fit in.

Now I've unpacked I feel the need to stretch my legs and explore a little, not so much to see the train itself but rather the folks who travel with me, For a watcher like me, public transport is a veritable banquet of insight on which to feast, a window of pleasure to study and dissect these creatures with whom I will share the track this evening.

Entering Carriage B there seems to be a bottleneck, a mix of folks waiting for the toilet, loading luggage into racks and lost souls still searching for their compartments so I unfold a window seat and perch to scratch my itch.

Straight ahead, sitting on a fold-down seat. Distinguished swept-back grey hair, middle-aged, no make-up but still very striking. Understated but expensive Belstaff overcoat. Sits confidently, self-assured. Writing something meaningful, lightly but quickly to someone important. Scents of Diptyque perfume. This is Civil Servant. Civil Servant likes André Rieu and non-fiction. She can afford a chauffeured Maybach but prefers the tube. She harbours a wild past that would shock her co-workers.

Skinny, slight man stood on my right shoulder. Grey, suede Adidas squash trainers. Faded cream chinos, slim-fitting nondescript charcoal jacket. Vacant look of boredom as if he's staring into a pond. Ordinary. This is Drained Leaf. Drained Leaf likes the middle of the spectrum, a lack of distinction, beigeness. He cares not for how he looks or the destination towards which his life choices are taking him. He is no one.

Slight stale scent on my immediate left. Six foot six. Brown corduroy trousers, long dank brown hair, battered skater trainers. Tatty, maroon T-shirt hanging from skeletal physique, unnecessary sunglasses for the time of day and setting. Ancient, second-generation iPhone. This is Grubby Ghoul. He likes that his unwashed hair attracts looks from people, and spends his days indulging himself in whatever takes him. He dislikes that he must rely on his mother for money when she represents societal conformity.

Immaculate skin, standing with her back to the door. Brunette hair pulled back into a tight ponytail. Cheap and sweet perfume, maybe Clinique. Brand new hot pink and black Lycra Nike yoga kit head to toe. Handbag says generic marketing bottom-feeder, badges on rucksack say she travelled once. New yoga mat cast carelessly by her feet suggests she's trying to be one of the girls but doesn't enjoy it. Small breasts. Foundation and lipstick match her gym gear. This is Try Hard. Try Hard likes many things that her girl group does not. Try Hard likes Dutch literature and hates exercise. Try Hard loves Toulouse-Lautrec paintings and dislikes marketing. Try Hard is dying.

Trains, buses, tubes and metros, endless combinations of human choices and shapes, colours and forms, all telling a story. It reminds of the H.G. Wells novel *The Time Machine*. In his future society the world is split into two kinds of creatures, Eloi and Morlocks. The Eloi are the superior form of the species; they live above ground in the pastured fields where the beating sun kisses their rosy cheeks and blond hair, and all they need is made and given to them by the Morlocks. The inferior creatures, Morlocks are wart-covered cretins, slaving away below ground in the dark, cavernous underworld with the steamy machinery.

Sounds like the traditional dichotomy that's explored in so many stories, but as Gary Sinise's character tells us in the movie *Ransom*, every once in a while Morlocks sporadically eat an Eloi.

CHAPTER 5

Isla

Back in my cabin, I absent-mindedly wander about the tiny space neatening things. Outside the bland fields and telegraph poles whip past the window as if on a carousel and remind me of a Hitchcock classic; as I turn around Bruno Anthony takes a seat at my tiny fold-down dining table and inches on a pair of black leather gloves before exclaiming, "How about Scotch and plain water, Clay? A pair. Doubles. The only kind of doubles I play!"

We're clear of London now and the scenery has already paled from the charged, bustle of the capital to the type of scenery that seems only visible from British train carriages; self-storage warehouses, the freight entrances to supermarkets lined with heavy goods vehicles and the overgrown gardens of those sorry, crowded terraced houses that back straight onto the railside fence.

The exercise tracker on my wrist that I purchased last week tells me that my resting heart rate is 33 beats per minute, which is easily within the range of an Olympic athlete. This is a fact I'm very proud of but also one which surprises me as it suggests that in no way am I excited about my destination. It's taken me a long time to get here, but frustration is not something I'm prone to so I'm just going to get comfortable.

I reach for my phone, open an internet browser window and select the bookmarked pages, my finger dancing up and down the screen exploring the list before I choose one and a hazy 1990s video fills the screen.

"Good morning and welcome to BBC News, I'm Kate Adie. The Hebridean village of Castlebay on the Isle of Barra in Scotland is today waking up to an outcry, a demand for answers that goes far beyond the island and was this morning raised in the House of Commons. How could such a travesty occur?"

Tap-tap. Someone is drumming fingernails on my door. I immediately lock my phone screen and pocket it.

"Hello?" I say in an uncertain voice, peering at the frosted glass window of my cabin door. All I can see is the dome of a child's head and a hand, fingers tapping on the window.

I lunge for the door, unlatch the lock and snatch it open, only to see two children running down the corridor giggling as they bustle beneath the legs of other passengers, in pursuit of their next prank.

Thundering away from London, gently bouncing with the motion of the tracks, my mind begins to wind backwards, back almost thirty years to my childhood and I momentarily feel an eerie sinking feeling, yet my tracker still insists my heart rate has not moved an inch and for a moment I'm convinced it has synchronised with the tempo of my Seamaster's tick. Good things come to those who wait.

I've left my door ajar to get some air moving through the cabin and I see a trainspotter shuffling down the slim corridor outside my room training an archaic old camera lens through the grimy window trying to capture lord knows what. I generally notice the glare of a lens in my immediate surroundings straight away; it's a result of being the focus of the collective lens of the British media at the age of six. Even now, at 35, to me the camera lens is the bend of a spider's leg to an arachnophobe. I avert my gaze out of the window; it's like an ever-changing painting, far greener now as we've shrugged London from our carriages and the Sleeper's wheels are making that rhythmic 'clickety clack' sound that children love to imitate. The motion of the rails cradles me, causing a very slight but repetitive bobbing. Up, down, left to right, left to right, up down.

It's a red sky tonight, one of those classic summer evenings that looks as if some god has plunged an unearthly wooden spoon into the treacle sky and slowly rotated it into a pool of swirls. This warm, lazy mood is smashed by the clatter of pots and the rustle of packets as the train attendant I met on the platform struggles past my door.

"Oh Jeezus! You startled me" she says, placing a hand across her chest to steady her heart. "I know you must be gasping for your brew but my bloody machine's run out of hot water so I've only made it to cabin seven," she explains with a jolliness that suggests she actually enjoys these little crises because it means she can chat with passengers more than usual. Her energetic work gives off a faint bodily smell. It's not sweat, so it must be a product she is wearing; it's more like a freshly struck match. So much so that I take a quick glance around to make sure this frantic girl isn't actually on fire.

"Ah, sod's law, hey," I reply, rolling my eyes and smiling.

"It sure is, my lovely. You're number 23," she says.

"That's me," I confirm. "Clay," I add with a smile.

"Well, fabulous to meet you again, Clay." There's a pause and I'm excited by the uncertainty of whether we're flirting or not.

"Now don't tell me; I pride myself on my memory," she says, jutting a hand into her hip, holding her forehead and looking to the sky. "Earl Grey no milk?"

"Oops, nearly," I say with a wink. "It was an English breakfast tea, no milk."

Her face falls, as if she's a little girl who's found herself standing on a West End stage before a sea of ogling eyes. She reanimates with a whip of her hand, grasps her trolley and returns to her journey. "OK, I'll be with you as soon as I can, lovely."

I look at her name tag again; it's still blank. "What's your name?" I ask.

"Ah, I'm Isla, lovely."

"Isla Lovely," I respond playfully. "Nice to meet you," I say, putting my feet up on the bunk ladder and grabbing the complimentary *Times* newspaper. Isla rushes off down the carriage corridor with a rattle and squeak of her trolley.

It was Earl Grey, no milk. I don't know why I do that.

This is Isla, I think to myself. I reckon Isla likes a cinnamon bun on her tea breaks and dislikes combing her hair. I think Isla likes her Scottish roots but felt a bite of wanderlust and so opted for a profession that would take her to different places, even if that only means Fort William, Glasgow, Carlisle, Crewe and London repeatedly on the Caledonian Sleeper. Isla bubbles with friendliness but her eyes are desperate, as if there's an invisible figure following her around. She's definitely carrying something.

I like Isla, I've decided.

CHAPTER 6

Doubt

My door bursts open with a crash!
"Excuse me!?" I bark, in a moment of high Britishness when it's this frantic young woman who's exploding into my cabin who should be asking to be excused. The fright of her entrance has knocked me back onto the bottom bunk of the bed and I lie there cowering but with an annoyed expression.
"Have you seen the lady I was with?"
"Wha–?"
"The lady! Miss Froy!" she interrupts me, speaking almost hysterically.
"Me? What?" I answer confusedly and feebly.
"But it's ridiculous, she took me to the dining car and came back with me," she presses, staring at me longingly for confirmation.
"You went, but came back alone," I'm shocked to hear myself answer.

The woman looks dumbfounded.

Then the sound of crockery rattling on a trolley comes from outside my cabin in the corridor and the woman swings around dramatically.

"You," she says, her accent high-pitched and upper class, "you served me tea just now!"

"Yes, Madame," says an attendant.

"Have you seen the lady l was with?" she fires back impatiently, desperate for acknowledgement.

"But Madame was alone," the attendant says solemnly as the train whooshes into a tunnel and its whistle blares out a wretched shriek.

The cabin continues to sway with the motion of the train but no one speaks in the darkness of the tunnel.

As we emerge from the black, I see my door is swinging closed. I try to shout "Wait!" but the lady vanishes.

CHAPTER 7

In Plain Sight

The train's constant motion is a comfort to a nomad like me.

It's sobering to think that, since the age of fifteen, my life and identity have been like the scenery I see rushing past my window, ever changing. In those twenty years I've lived in eleven different British towns and eighteen different homes. In the earlier years of hiding when I was in my late teens, I grew nervous easily and so I kept on the move. When I first met people I kept to the bare essentials for a British conversation which is basically name, where I came from and the football team I supported. But if I'd stumble, maybe on the school I attended or my father's occupation, I'd panic and uproot and that would be another one added to the long list of relocations.

Today I'm far more composed and am happy to report I've been in London for eight years where I have a job, what people may call a "partner" and a cluster of "friends", none of whom have any idea who I am. All they know is I am called Clay and I'm assistant concierge at the Corinthia Hotel near Embankment. They know I love the Italian dessert caramel panna cotta and dislike people who feel the need to speak during movies. Aside from that, they simply know a set of facts that I've fed to them. That is all. It doesn't take as much effort to maintain nowadays. I've gotten into a rhythm with it. Much like the motion of this Caledonian Sleeper.

The need to frequently change my identity to preserve my safety has meant that I've become an expert about so many British towns. When I was entered into the protection programme my original legend was that I was from Glasgow in my native Scotland but as I encountered my first "risk of identification" or ROI, I was forced to switch and so chose Northern England as I found the accent easiest. Since then I've been a Geordie, a Scouser, a Corkian and a Cockney. Today I maintain a neutral, unremarkable middle-England accent. The grey man.

I'll always remember my first ROI. I was seventeen and living in the coastal town of Hull in England's north-east. I had just completed my first day in a soulless job as a telemarketer selling kitchens one January when the team invited me out for a drink. We were sitting in the Haworth Arms on Beverley Road when a news report on the

TV mounted in the corner mentioned that the anniversary of Scotland's Darkest Day, 7th January, was approaching. The table started discussing it.

"Absolutely horrific, wasn't it?" someone began.

"Tragic," said a young woman.

"Unspeakable," said a bespectacled man.

"There was a survivor, wasn't there?" asked the middle-aged manager of the group, sipping his ale.

"Yeah he…"

"Or she!" another young man interjected.

"… was given a new identity. Too much attention around the case and he – or she!" the manager said with upturned palms to indicate gender inclusivity "was a minor."

"You hardly ever hear of that…" said a woman of about thirty-five. "Kids just being whisked away and their identity changed after an incident."

The manager flicked up his eyebrows, closed his eyes and nodded slowly in agreement, lifting his pint to his lips to take another sip.

"There were a couple of cases in the eighties and nineties if memory serves," he continued. "James Bulger, right? I reckon it's only done for certain cases which involve youngsters and national media attention, mind."

"Kind of creepy though, isn't it?" the young girl said, staring up at the TV screen. "That they're just out there in society. Walking among us."

"I'm not sure about *creepy*," said another team member. "A survivor of Scotland's Darkest Day is probably psychologically scarred beyond belief; it's

only right they're given a fresh start I reckon."
I don't know why but one of the girls in the group, a manager from another team, wouldn't stop staring at me and the more she did the quieter I became, forgetting all of my training to never clam up and always embrace the conversation about "Classroom B". Later that evening she approached me at the bar and began drunkenly probing.

"Do you know something about all that?" she asked. "You looked pretty anxious when the group was talking about it earlier. Maybe I'm overthinking this and I know you said you were from Crewe, but every so often you say a word proper Scottish like." She was stumbling through the words after four glasses of pub white wine but she was managing to deliver her question and it frightened me.

I laughed it off and plied her with more drinks in the hope she'd have no memory of even being at the Haworth let alone interrogating me. I spent the next three weeks trying to be more sociable and even faked a mutual interest in her obsession with Ken Follett novels to paint over any memory she had of me as awkward or withdrawn and snuff out any suspicions.

At the end of the month I moved on to the next town to start again.

Since leaving Castlebay I've had numerous partners but no relationship.
I've had countless friends but no connections.

I've lived in plenty of houses but never a home. I've held numerous jobs but had no career.

Running from that event in Classroom B all of these years has left me faceless. I imagine I'm quite unremarkable to you. Simple Clay, that's me. Part of the vast army of the faceless British general public, a prole if you will. My banality places me at the largest point on any bell curve chart, with the rest of the nondescript masses, so the chances are you've walked past me in the street, perhaps even this evening, you on your way home from work, me on my way to catching this train.

CHAPTER 8

Setting Sail for a New Life

I may mask it but underneath, I am proud to be from the Isle of Barra off the coast of bonnie Scotland. Barra is part of the Outer Hebrides. It is about six miles wide and eleven long; the length varies depending on the time of day and tides. You've probably never heard of Barra, not many have. If you've ever scribbled the outline of the United Kingdom, you've never drawn Barra, it's a true spit of land that's rarely even visualised on the weather forecaster's screen.

British people have a saying when implying great remoteness or painful distance: "It's only round the corner, it's not as if it's the Outer Hebrides!" Another which I heard the other day was "I'd get rid of the cheating prick, banish the bastard to the Outer Hebrides!" I only became aware of these turns of phrase after I'd left Barra; ironically the island is too remote to have heard such mainland phrases while growing up.

You can reach the scuttling little town by one of two means. The ferry nestles in the docks three times a day and serves not just Castlebay but the thirteen other hamlets and towns scattered across Barra. The second option, for those with a pretty penny to spend, is by plane. Let me be clear that, when I say plane, I do not mean a 737 airliner, nor do I mean any other sort of plane which your mind will have fetched from airport memories. When I say plane, I refer to the terrifyingly named Island Hopper. A collection of tin-like panels riveted together, a single lonely propeller eagerly dragging its body through the sky, the inside of which is covered in a coarse grey carpet from floor to ceiling. The Island Hopper lands on the beach. Yes, it *lands* on the beach, and during high tides the "runway" disappears altogether beneath the waves. I am forever incredulous when describing Barra's airport. I've never opted for this mode of transport and never will due to a fear that the vicious Scottish wind will pluck it from the clouds and swallow it into the ocean. Each day one plane takes off at six and returns at four and I have nothing but admiration for the eight souls onboard who call it their commute; they're braver people than me. Or just stupid.

When I lived there, Castlebay boasted a throbbing population of 1,003 but that's more than enough when a solid 1,000 of them hate your family. Physically speaking it's an enchanting town which seems to be comfortably nestling in a crescent around the harbour but also seems to be clinging to the island's rock face for dear life at the same time. Beautiful but precarious. The island does not immediately strike you as cradling the houses and church so much as tolerating them. At times the dwellings even seem to quiver, being so close to the water's edge, but it's a trade-off made by their owners for the opportunity to have such an astounding coastal view every morning. The centrepiece of this ornamental town is Kisimul Castle which is set about 170 yards off the harbour, surrounded by sea. As castles go it's pretty tiny, a short keep jutting out of squat walls wrapped around a courtyard like two fat arms. Made from ancient stone and dappled with swampy green moss it has an access path that emerges menacingly from the sea like a monster's tongue penetrating the portcullis.

It may be small but that didn't erode my obsession with it as a young boy. Its granite walls were built somewhere around the thirteenth century, it was the seat of the MacNeil Clan and said to be utterly impregnable. Kisimul Castle is the one vision in life that my mind does not liken to a movie scene or backdrop. There is nothing in existence like it.

Sitting in the mouth of the Atlantic, it is this treacherous town which is the destination of my trip tonight.

"Still a few months off yet, lad, you're not

ready" was the repeated response from Bernie, my protection officer throughout the summer of 2001. She'd become increasingly more direct in her delivery with each week that went by, a feature of her training, to mature her subject, which was me. I'd been disappointed. At sixteen years old I'd been in the Vulnerable Persons Protection Programme training for almost six years, living at my Uncle Gordon's on the neighbouring island of Hellisay. I'd worked hard on my legend, feeling a sense of obligation to maintain it to a high standard for my strange, mismatched, surrogate parents Bernadette Cruikshank and Faisel Shepherd. Bernie and Fiz. They sound like a bad 90s children's TV show.

I pined to leave the Hebridean Island of Hellisay and for my Uncle Gordon to develop an uncharacteristic adventurous side, urging me to seize the day and set off on my journey. But ever fearful of conflict he gently and calmly talked me down from leaving each time.

It was a hellishly cold evening on Hellisay in winter that same year when I decided to do it, to leave. He'd just finished his evening ritual of preparing a fire, playing his daily chess move in the game he and I maintained on the corner table in the pyramid window, before retreating to his alcove den to give me "my space" and read his Icelandic sagas. He dropped off to sleep just before one o'clock in the morning and I climbed the stairs to my room. The staircase was a breathtaking half spiral which coiled around the wall of the cottage. Carved from a 400-year-old oak it was a single piece of master carpentry, but at that moment its defining feature was that the lack of joints and fixings meant it did not make a single creak as I tentatively climbed it to the first floor.

I hurried to my room and found my bag. Uncle Gordon never set foot in there so there was no need to hide it. I'd spent the previous week slowly siphoning clothes and other items to pack each night. A surreal and quite intimidating act. I think most of us have packed a "runaway" bag as children; it's usually an exciting and slightly comical process involving your favourite teddy, chocolate-coated snack and ridiculous equipment for surviving in the world like an umbrella and off you go. This time however, while exciting it was not comical, it was sobering. What do you take with you when you're never coming back? The vastness of the world out there was overwhelming. I'd decided on intense practicality. I had a selection of carefully chosen clothes based on size and warmth along with my watch and some toiletries. I'd left the most important thing until tonight. I slid out of my bedroom and listened for confirmation that Uncle Gordon was still asleep. I entered the bathroom and reached behind the sink, loosened the panel and tensed my arm as I slid it inside, half expecting to feel sickening legs crawling over my fingers. After patting my hand left and right a few times, my fingers brushed the delicate and smooth strains of my Castlebay Primary School sanderling feather. I clutched its stem and carefully reversed my hand out. Returning to my room, I slid my treasure inside a book and I was ready.

I left the house at 03:00, released Uncle Gordon's boat from the tiny jetty and made my way across the bay to Barra where the Castlebay Ferry terminal awaited. I was off to start again. Off to leave the Kinkade name behind. Leave the hatred and vitriol behind. Leave my neglectful mum Rhona behind. Leave ghostly Uncle Gordon behind. Leave my classmates Kerin, Simone, Jack and little Bobo behind.

That morning, the crescent-shaped Castlebay vista was like a scene from *Midsommar*; a stark and shocking contrast. The green slopes framing clean white buildings and hanging baskets bursting with coloured pansies should – as with the ethereal Scandinavian vistas in the film – conjure feelings of joy and innocence. But instead Castlebay, like the movie, was contrapuntal, emanating an aura of unspeakable horror, a force more sinister than one can imagine.

"07:13 to Oban!" a tiny, neckerchiefed and grimy man announced.

I remember thinking, "The legend begins today."

When I left Castlebay, it was to escape persecution

from the events of 7th January 1991 but also because of a sense of awe courtesy of Universal, MGM and Paramount Pictures. Films beckoned me to the dazzling worlds that awaited if I could only muster the courage. Now older and wiser I realise that fixation was and is rooted in escapism. I found it the perfect remedy for any of the numerous challenges a child encounters growing up. A bout of the Sunday night blues? Just watch *Pippi Longstocking*. Missing your absent father? Lose yourself in *American Beauty*. Feeling poorly? Grab *Rear Window*. Homework too tough? Have a day off with Ferris Bueller.

Your local community is pouring hatred on your family? That one took a little more than movies to address.

I'm startled as the old speaker in a wooden box on the wall crackles to life again.

"Good evening," says a bodiless and yet intimate voice. I am expecting a generic, pre-recorded message but am delighted when I realise the passenger address is live. The speaker clears her throat.

"We're so grateful you chose to travel with us this evening, we're now free of London and are making our way steadily towards Crewe."

Her voice seems stilted and overly formal, like a 1990s newsreader.

"After which we will press on and – if the journey is without delay – cross the border to Scotland as the clock strikes twelve." The phrasing of this time of the day makes me chuckle to myself, but this stops as the speaker's voice takes on a notably lower tone. As she begins to describe the journey towards Fort William and the onward travel options available for those wanting to reach the Hebrides, her speech slows and there's an undeniable tone of dread. I begin to question whether it's just me who can hear this or whether others are registering it too. Her voice contorts around the words, manhandles them from her mouth, and at one point I'm genuinely worried she's having a stroke.

As the voice slowly drains away, thanks passengers and signs off I realise it belongs to Isla, the carriage attendant.

CHAPTER 9

Replicants

A hunger stirs within me, partly for food but mainly to watch and so I leave my cabin in search of faces and it's not long before I happen upon one of the train's many broad, panoramic windows which run the length of some carriages. The world flashes by these endless windows in elongated bars of sliding colour. People naturally stop and gather to watch the show. We fly in and out of tunnels, past pulsing signal lights, all the while the high-pitched rushing noise of air through gaps in the train's body battering your ears. The Caledonian Sleeper company has attempted to further dress the experience of these panoramic windows with small fairy lights running along the ceiling. While these are completely at odds with the rest of the traditional mise en scène aboard the train, for me it accentuates a feeling that I'm on board a craft circling Los Angeles in dystopian 2019 looking for replicants with Harrison Ford.

There's a man with his back to the window, like he's trying to avoid being interested by the striking landscape whooshing by. His frame is bear-like. Like one solid lump of matter. It gives the impression that things move around him as he traverses the world rather than him navigating them. He's olive skinned, under six foot, which accentuates his stockiness, and dressed impeccably in a casual double-breasted burgundy wool jacket, cream chinos and loafers. And there's a steeliness about his eyes; think Stanley Tucci in *Margin Call*. He winks at me without smiling and I smile flirtatiously in response. This is Sullen Bear. He likes controlling every moment of his day and dislikes being in groups where he is not commanding the conversation. Sullen Bear is only on this train because he read about it in *GQ*, and is already disappointed.

Standing alone, two feet from him, is a young woman, perhaps thirty years old. I cannot see her face as she is enraptured by the light show darting by the panoramic window. She's slim and tall. Shimmering, conditioned brunette hair. Oversized but stylish lightweight lambswool cardigan, fitted blue jeans and penny loafers. So struck by the view is she that her elegant hand is laid open-palm across the glass, nails manicured and glossy. She's trying to touch the view, but cannot. She moves with graceful purpose but sharpened self-awareness. This is Silent Siren. She likes being near the ocean because crashing waves is the sound she remembers most clearly; she dislikes speakers of any kind. She turns from the window to leave and extracts a lip balm from her handbag. As she applies it her finger tidies her hair behind her ear and I see her hearing aid.

Detective Rick Deckard appears at my shoulder. "Replicants, they're more human than human itself, right?"

CHAPTER 10

Whisky Galore

Seagulls are calling outside the train. Are they following me back to the coast? I watch as they gather in a messy flock alongside the speeding train, flashes of white clawing through the air in front of the ever-diminishing sun.

I reach for the minibar to investigate whether its contents are as charmingly old-fashioned as the rest of the train's surroundings and I'm not disappointed. The small fridge offers no recognisable brand names, no generic mainstream gin or mass-produced vodka, just obscure and unique miniature glass bottles. I reach for a small bottle of whisky named The Covenanter. The label features the Scottish historical figure Alexander Peden, a charismatic preacher who wore a horrific mask of leather and human hair as a disguise to avoid arrest for preaching illegally. I sit back, turn the small metal screw cap and lift the neck to my nose. The rich and harsh malty smell of whisky shoots up my nostrils and swirls gently in that indescribable chamber between your nose and ears and I close my eyes.

Castlebay is full of tales, both myth and reality. A particularly enchanting and true story occurred off the coast of Barra and is dramatised in Compton Mackenzie's novel *Whisky Galore*. A cargo ship called the SS *Politician* left Liverpool in 1941 headed for Jamaica and it hit rocks off the coast of the neighbouring Hebridean island of Eriskay. Everyone survived as they were so close to our islands but it tipped its whole load into the sea. We're talking money, food, building materials... and whisky. With the ration restrictions of wartime still tightly around the throats of the islanders, when they got word that barrels of whisky were bobbing around in their bay they were into the water faster than a school of lifeguards. Legend has it the men donned women's dresses to avoid getting incriminating ship oil on their clothes, because by recovering the hooch they were thieving. I still like to imagine all those little islanders diving for barrels during stormy winds and returning with their own batch of the nectar that they'd been denied for so long. But the bit I love most about the story is that those locals recovered all the surviving whisky consignment from the wreckage, but only three-quarters of it was returned to the customs officers. So, somewhere out there, some lucky souls have a bottle of SS *Polly* 1941 in their cellar, gathering dust and value by the second. Today a bottle is worth just over £81,000.

All of this makes Castlebay one of the gems of the British Isles. A gem to visit that is; when you're ten years old and you live there all year round, it becomes immensely beige and even Kisimul Castle was taken for granted.

After weaving myself into the myriad of humans in London for my latest legend, I have learned that "remote and bloody cold" aren't the only adjectives to describe Castlebay. Whenever the awful anniversary of that day appeared on TV each January and the bay was splashed on every prime-time screen in the UK, I'd hear people swoon over images of the bobbing fishing boats and the "majestic land" from which I secretly hail. I'd feel a pang of something, not quite homesickness, rather just sickness, a flint-like taste at the back of my mouth like that which arrives after being punched in the temple.

CHAPTER 11

Hunted

We're passing Northampton. Or Milton Keynes. I can't tell. The pre-dinner aperitif has its desired effect as my surroundings soften and my head still swims in the whisky-laced waters of Castlebay. My body and mind have now become fully acclimated to the motion and I have all but forgotten I am on a train thundering across the country. The whisky delivers a playfulness now and I decide to feed it with a walk through the carriages.

The corridors smell different to my cabin, the ill-fitting windows allow the outside air to gush in through small spaces giving the train the scent of whichever district it's passing through. I'm unsure where in the country we are exactly but I do know that it's rural as the manure smell is heavy. Lazy violin music plays over the speakers mounted in the corners of each corridor.

I'm walking in the direction of travel. As I wander my pace is sporadically quickened with fleeting surges in the train's motion. I enter what I count is the fourth carriage from my cabin and see a small bank of wooden telephone vestibules. There are three in a row, each with their own candlestick telephone where the user must hold the cup-like piece to their ear and speak into the microphone mounted on a stick affixed to the wall. Sat on top of each vestibules are small bird carvings, maybe falcons.

One of the phones is occupied by a short, middle-aged man in a well-tailored, single-breasted grey suit and beige trench coat wearing a brown trilby hat. He is facing away from me, his chin tucked into his chest and the earpiece grasped tightly to the side of his head by a bunch of swollen fingers. I slow my steps to try to eavesdrop on his conversation but I cannot hear above the clattering train wheels and constant high-pitched blowing of air through gaps in the windows. I decide to pick up the phone to his right and feign dialling. It is as I'm trying to understand the antique phone that I feel a hand on my shoulder and swing around in fright.

"YOU!" growls the man in the hat, his long teeth resting on his lip and eyebrows frowning above eyes that have clearly seen much terror over the years.

"Have you seen *him*!?" he continues in an aggressive interrogatory voice.

"Who?" I say, startled, pushing myself back into the vestibule.

The man steps back to give me some more space. He tiredly removes his hat and runs a hand through lacquered 1940s-style hair and wipes the back of his neck with a handkerchief.

"I've been looking for him for years," continues the man in a weary tone, his body heavy with exhaustion as he leans against the phone booth, sweeps his coat over his hip and rests his fist there. I can smell cigar smoke and my eyes search his other hand for anything burning but don't find it. The carriage music from the crackling speakers has begun a slow, stabbing oboe rhythm.

"Don't play dumb with me, kid; you know, everyone knows. We're all looking for him, but..." He exhales and the disappointment from years of fruitless searching seeps from him. "He's a damn ghost, he's a ghost, I tell ya."

My throat begins to close with panic and I struggle to stop my eyes from widening with terror. I say nothing.

"If you see him, you give me a call, ya hear?" He hands me his card and places the hat back on his head. His card reads 'Sam Spade'.

"You getting this, son, or am I going too fast for ya?"

I'm still speechless with shock. Is he looking for me? Have I finally been found?

"I hope they don't hang you, precious, by that sweet neck." He walks past me and I wait for a second before I dare turn around to steal another look, but when I do he's already gone.

CHAPTER 12

Rhona Kinkade

The encounter with the man, the detective, the private investigator, whatever the hell he was, has rattled me and so I return briskly to my cabin for the security that comes from solitude. Sitting in the small chair stuffed beneath the upper bunk, I pull a blanket over myself, less for comfort and more as a pathetic form of camouflage and I think of home. Thinking of Castlebay.

Our house could have come straight from the mind of Tolkien. A knackered, cosy cottage with sagging beams and sagging thatched roof. It had been there, at the end of the Brevig track, for such an age that it no longer seemed man-made because there weren't enough angles or straight lines remaining. It was named The Craigard and had fully set root, a true hobbit house in The Shire, a little home carved from the earth. But while we lived in this remote nursery-rhyme dwelling we weren't too far from the Clach Mhile shop where I would be sent to collect brandy snaps for my sweet-toothed mum, a teacher at the village school.

We moved to Castlebay in 1990 when I was four as part of a downsizing exercise. The cause of this relocation was pretty depressing; On Wednesday 5th October 1988 my father boarded his fishing trawler the *Björgey*, set his coordinates for his favourite pocket of North Sea where he usually struck cod-shaped gold and set off as he had for most of his working life. Dad never came home. His demise was described differently depending on who you spoke to in Fraserburgh. "Alan went doing what he loved doing, chasing scales."

"He was taken by the sea was that one."

"He liked a wee dram so he did."

"October was very stormy that year, God rest him."

Regardless of which local gossip to which you subscribed, my old man was the victim of Mother Nature. Parts of the *Björgey* were found way up in the Norwegian Sea but the general consensus is that the archaic trawler couldn't withstand the particularly bad Nordic storms that Wednesday night and he went down with his vessel.

So, with a young mouth to feed mum secured a job at Castlebay Primary and moved us to The Craigard. With time I began to question how exactly Mum stumbled across that job, as the remoteness of the isle suggests you'd need to actively seek opportunities there. Today, whenever my eyes slowly track the 314-mile journey on a map between Fraserburgh and Castlebay I am resigned to the thought that Mum couldn't bear the grief of being near the place she'd shared with Dad and simply had to get us far away.

I've not seen my mum since I left the Isle of Barra. The trauma of Scotland's Darkest Day caused her to have a breakdown and she was committed to a hospital in Oban on the west coast of the Scottish mainland before her trial.

Eighteen months after the incident in January 1991 she was found guilty of gross negligence but mentally unstable and so for the last twenty-nine years she's been at that psychiatric unit in the Highlands. Her face has almost faded completely from my memory now.

The terms of my protection mean I'm not permitted to hold pictures or evidence of my root life and so all I have are the blurry stills in my head from childhood.

Stills of her kneeling down to help a classmate with their finger painting.

Stills of her applauding a classmate with one hand on her thigh as she holds a younger one on her hip. Stills of her caring for everyone around her. Putting them all before herself. And me.

That was my mum Rhona. Mum liked dipping brandy snaps in double cream and disliked large shipwrecks when viewed from the surface because the scale of them gave her vertigo and a feeling of insignificance. Mum liked the skin from chicken but disliked chicken. She liked the endorphins released in her body when something she was naturally good at made someone's life easier, and she disliked the slow loris as they always appeared to be worrying.

Isla flashes by my compartment's open door and jolts me from my pensive mood.

"Ahoy there, Clay!" she says comically, dashing down the corridor with a fish-like swiftness leaving a trail of sugar packets and those little wooden stirrers strewn along the floor, a task she'll likely blame on careless passengers during her next visit, I think.

"Keep going, Isla!" I encourage while enjoying how her apron draws her waist tight and accentuates her full bum in the Caledonian company trousers that are clearly a size too small. I begin to look forward to seeing her again.

I look up and down the carriage but there's no sign of the investigator in the trilby.

CHAPTER 13

Spying

I'm walking the carriages again but don't remember leaving my cabin. I'm unsure as to where in the country we are now. The swaying of the carriage and relentless motion without any stops for the last three hours has induced a womb-like state. I'm being carried by this train, to an inevitable end.

The air rushing through the window cracks has become colder, a distinctive mix of the everyday things that seem to exhale when the sun has gone down, like tarmac and trees. They're only perceptible after the beating heat has ceased. A glance at my timepi– at my watch suggests it's been two hours since we left London. That cannot be. Seamasters are not known for their faulty timekeeping but I am convinced we've only been on board for twenty minutes.

Up ahead is a luggage car. It's open at both

ends with old steel bars and tired leather straps providing storage racks up its walls and across its ceiling. As I approach it I can see a woman standing anxiously, scanning over her shoulders, and I dash into a small conductor's vestibule on the left-hand side. A perfect opportunity to scratch my itch and study her.

She's in the shadows, barely lit save for the solitary lightbulb and its metal chain cord that swings violently overhead as the train jerks. She appears to be waiting. Waiting until it's clear? Waiting to do something? Waiting for someone? I feel a throb of excitement in my chest and a swelling of pleasure down below.

She's checked her watch four times in the twenty seconds since I concealed myself and just as I am about to approach her there are footsteps behind me and I cower in the vestibule hoping I'm not seen. From my crouched position, I see the legs of a black-clothed athletic man walk purposefully past me and into the luggage car. The speaker in the corner of the ceiling overhead begins playing moody, staccato pops from a trumpet which make me sizzle with a feeling of espionage. He seizes the woman by her biceps, not in an aggressive way, but protective, concerned, and she seems to melt, uttering the word "James" in a Russian accent. They begin a hushed discussion which I strain to hear.

SLAM. A window crashes open and frightens me. The wind is screaming into the carriage now and the man dashes to close it, checking up and down the corridor with laser focus. I cannot believe he hasn't seen me. The sudden gust of air has made the carriage momentarily colder and industrial smells linger in the air from the town we're passing through. Perhaps a metalworks.

The man returns to the woman and she looks down solemnly at a traditionally styled brown leather suitcase – I hadn't seen that a moment ago. The man dips down onto one knee and inspects it as if it's made of glass, delicately curling his fingers around its corners and studying its handle and hinges. Then in one swift motion he grasps the case, tucks it beneath his arm and turns around to face the storage area on the wall. The woman lunges and grabs his arm, he turns and kisses her firmly and the pair sink into each other.

The speaker has begun to play a long-noted, cinematic string piece now. As quickly as the pair embraced, they're apart again and I realise the man is not storing the bag, he's climbing the rack and reaching for a hatch in the ceiling. After two pushes he finally pries it open and slings the heavy wooden panel upwards and over its hinges where it crashes onto the carriage roof. He presses the suitcase against his chest with one hand and scampers up the rack like an insect, and just before disappearing into the black void in the ceiling he turns to look at the woman one last time. Then he's gone. The roof hatch is replaced, the train back to its gentle swaying, the storage straps flapping against the steel racks and the woman standing beneath the swinging lightbulb, silently weeping into her hands.

CHAPTER 14

The Five Friends

This train feels filmic. It feels like I'm walking through scenes not carriages and this transports me back to being a child. As I wander down the carriage I hear giggles; a child's giggles. Unsure as to whether they're coming from up ahead or behind I stop abruptly and try to force my ears to widen. The giggles are echoing, and then crackling. I look up and am convinced the bodiless noises are coming through the speaker in the box on the ceiling. I approach it and strain to get nearer.

As I stand trying to confirm my suspicion, a group of little children, some toddlers, some older darts beneath my legs, barging at each other and chattering happily in lively Scottish accents. They disappear through the door to the next carriage and out of sight, yet their playful voices seem to return to the speaker on the ceiling, crackling distantly.

I arrive at my cabin feeling a little less jovial. Those little native accents are stirring things in me.

Such was the size of Castlebay, the local school housed just two classrooms, Room A and Classroom B. One may assume that this is how students of different ages were separated for different curriculums when in reality Castlebay seldom had enough children for two rooms and so Room A had become a chaotic storage room of fishing equipment for which the local fisherman gave the school minuscule financial contributions each year. Classroom B was where actual classes happened and today the label has become a synonym of dread, a touchstone for utter horror.

I made friends quickly as a child. Whether it was the lack of a father figure which over-developed my social sensitivity or the lack of any siblings which made me crave companionship I would work the classroom with relative success. In my class, taught in Classroom B, there was me, Kerin, Simone, Bobo and Jack. We were all between the ages of four and seven.

Kerin Peacock was one of the oldest of the group at seven years old. She had mousy brown, thin hair and was most frequently referred to as a "little madam" due to her constant insistence on being right, first in line, taller, funnier, or more of an islander than anyone else who'd ever lived. Kerin liked her mum to slightly overcook rice so that it formed a skin that required peeling from the pan and disliked newcomers to the island, seeing them as fresh subjects who must be educated on all of her superiorities.

Simone Stott was six and the very epitome of Scotch. She had pale, milky skin peppered with freckles, not just those sun-blemished cute ones that straddle the bridge of the nose, but the head-to-toe kind that are reserved for the red-headed race. Simone's eyes were like kaleidoscopes, they continually twinkled and burst with colour. She was a miniature barrel of energy, constantly running, gesticulating or shouting. Likely a sufferer from hyperactivity, Simone liked being told she could not touch, press, switch or pull something. Her body would shudder with excitement before her limbs burst like a firework and she ran to the prohibited button, handle or cord. Simone disliked any food whose origin was not on the island, leading to her mother conjuring elaborate stories about Barra's avocado farms and lush orange groves.

Bobo, aged five and really called Isobel, was named after her grandma, who was the smallest woman I'd ever seen, a fact frequently debated by Kerin who insisted the smallest woman I'd ever seen was *actually* the Toffee Taster at the Barra Toffee Factory. Grandma Isobel was white-haired, demure and graceful. She'd married a soldier just before the Second World War whose speech had been damaged by a bomb in a Belgian village and after two years of him saying "Bobo" when he wanted his whisky poured she realised that was her new name and soon the entire family referred to her as Nana Bobo. My classmate Isobel Winkle was so close to her grandma that she demanded she be called the same. I always felt Bobo was the name of a clumsy, cumbersome person, a trombone player, an indulgent baker. Little Bobo was none of these things; she was as tiny as her Nana Bobo. She had thin auburn hair which was held off her petite infantile features with a delicate diamante hair clasp. Bobo lived in a world of her own, chatting to herself or her doll, or her neighbour's dog, a stranger's dog, an inanimate object. Anything was a potential recipient of some adorable Bobo chatter.

Bobo liked watching the sun climb over the hill across their vast back garden early each morning and disliked nothing.

Jack Hutch was four, the youngest and quietest of the bunch. He had an obsession with trains, and while this is not unlike countless boys of his age, Jack's awe of the machines was intensified by the fact that Barra does not have one foot of railway line and so there are no trains. The women of the island would swoon and coo at the sight of him inching into a room. "Ooo, you know what, Jeannie, he's gonna be a wee heartbreaker, isn't he?" They were right. Jack was a perfect-looking boy, with blond hair that sprouted from the exact centre of his crown and lay shimmering against his small round head which was often covered with a flat train driver's cap. Jack barely spoke, but when he arrived at a classmate's birthday party, of which there were four every year, the mums would have colluded to ensure there was a steam engine toy somewhere in the garden or living room for him to find. Jack would eventually loosen his grip on his mother's forearm which he clutched against his chest and make a beeline for the toy the moment he saw it. He would then navigate the party, bear-hugging the train, silently surveying the revelry safe in the knowledge that *he* had the train.

Jack liked the scent from the nook of his mum's neck and eating tuna mayonnaise; he disliked loud noises and being left alone.

There was only one other child of school age and that was Jack's big sister Sorrell. She was slightly older than the rest of us at ten and so represented a challenge. Sorrell and Jack's mother Karen was insistent that she should have personal tutoring and that, as the only teacher on the island, my mum Rhona would have to provide Sorrell with a healthy spread of English, Maths and History, "and some instrument guidance if you have time?" Karen would enquire hopefully. But Sorrell still came and sat in class with us younglings just to get out of the house, and this is where I became enchanted by her.

As a little boy you're not sure what the feeling is. It's not the sexual charge you feel when you've reached adolescence, it's more of an idolisation. A warm, sweet, gooey feeling when you're near the person. Our first ever interaction was more of a dusting off. She picked me up off the floor after I'd scuffled with Simone. I can still smell Sorrell's hair. It was like linen and apples and bright purple. I'm fully aware purple doesn't have a smell, but it did when she scooped me off my back and dumped me back on my feet.

This is Sorrell: Sorrell recited memorised phone numbers while on the toilet to distract her mind from the local myth of toilet trolls. Sorrell loved to use her hands and constantly had paint or pencil lead across her fingertips. Sorrell liked local history and disliked the thought of leaving Scotland for anywhere else in the world.

Sorrell and I became closer in my first years in Castlebay, playing and exploring the hills around the bay whenever I came to her lodge to meet mum after she'd tutored Sorrell. I thought of her all the time after the Classroom B tragedy; her family left the island almost immediately after the investigations had finished. I assume it was simply too painful to stay. In recent years I've toyed with the idea of looking her up, but that kind of thing is strictly against the rules and so instead I'll do what I always do; unlock my phone screen, open the internet browser and click play on the YouTube video which is bookmarked; the video has 34,506 views. I must be responsible for thirty thousand of those, I think to myself.

"From the headquarters of ITN, a special bulletin with Martyn Lewis.

"Good afternoon and welcome to the programme.

The 7th of January 1991 will never be forgotten; those were the words of Prime Minister John Major during a press conference outside 10 Downing Street today where he spoke of the horror that has befallen the fishing town Castlebay on the Isle of Barra in Scotland."

CHAPTER 15

God's Lonely Man

I awake from a light sleep in my cabin, surprised that my body required an impromptu nap, but I reassure myself it's the result of the cognitive load on my brain. The processing of what is to come.

"What a journey this is," I utter to myself softly as I rub my eyes and get the blood flowing back through my cold feet.

"You talkin' to me?" a male voice says from across the cabin and I jump back in my seat beneath the bunk in fright.

The voice belongs to a wiry, shirtless man pointing an enormous Magnum handgun in my face.

"Well, I'm the only one here... Who the fuck do you think you're talking to?" he presses.

His fine brown hair is swept over his pale, angular face. The strong smell of bitter coffee lingers.

"Hey Travis," I reply, in the tone of an old friend,

"how about getting that gun out of my face?"

He lies down awkwardly on my bunk.

"What are you doing here?" I ask, pouring myself a drink.

"I ride around most nights – subways, buses – but you know, if I'm gonna do that I might as well get paid for it." From somewhere, elongated trumpets fade in slowly while a drum taps quickly and then slows, speeds up again and then slows.

"I hear ya," I reply. "I'm a bit of a wanderer too. I've been doing it for years now."

He lies on my bunk, staring at the ceiling, his hands cupping the back of his head. "The days can go on with regularity over and over, one day indistinguishable from the next. A long continuous chain. Then suddenly, there is a change."

"Well, that's certainly true for me," I say. "I've decided to take action, that's the reason I'm on this train. I left home twenty years ago, Travis. I've lived all over, met so many people but I don't really know anyone, and they definitely don't know me."

"Loneliness has followed me my whole life," Travis retorts, "…everywhere. In bars, in cars, sidewalks, stores, everywhere. There's no escape. I'm God's lonely man."

I sip my drink, listening intently.

"Now I see this clearly," Travis says. "My whole life is pointed in one direction".

I stand and lean on the window, looking into the passing night. I don't need to turn around. I know there's nobody in the room with me.

CHAPTER 16

A New Legend in Training

There's a slight knock at my door and despite it being a very delicate tap, the flimsy material means the door flexes in its frame. There's a sharp jab of a violin somewhere and a voice whispers, "Vertigo".

"I've your tea, lovely." There's a particular type of person who refers to people with the adjective 'lovely', and Isla is that type. The violin disappears and I feel a buzz in my stomach.

"Ah, you're a star, Isla, thank you."

"Well!" she exhales, leaning against the door in an exaggerated manner to accentuate her exhaustion. "It's just one of those nights tonight, it really is."

There is a glisten on her forehead; all this hard work is activating her antiperspirant giving me smells of honey, spices and lavender.

"I can't imagine keeping us all fed and watered

while we cross the length of the UK; it's a long old shift I imagine."

"It is, it is," she agrees with a contented smile that tells me that, despite its demands, she loves her job.

"...but I love it," she confirms, "it keeps me busy, my mind busy." She dabs her sweaty brow with the back of her hand which is covered in written notes of some kind. She's looking for an excuse to rest and I decide to grant it to her. I can't help but think she looks younger than when I saw her last, rushing past my room.

"Lovely changing scenery your job provides though." I nod towards the window.

"That it does, that it does," she agrees, elongating the "does" and dipping her head to peer over my shoulder out of the window.

"My little brother was obsessed with trains," I say. This is a lie; I have no siblings. "He'd have loved working on board the Caledonian Sleeper!"

She seems hesitant for a moment and then responds. "Yes, it is a magical one isn't it? We've 71 aboard tonight but only four Islas to get them all fed!" She titters, blinking her eyes towards the ceiling like a schoolgirl looking for encouragement.

"Good grief! I don't envy you."

"Are you visiting or heading home?" she enquiries, adjusting her apron. "I thought there was a whiff of a Highlands accent in there, maybe even further north..." She's testing that wit of hers again.

"Ah no, just visiting. I'm from all over really but I have family up in Scotland and so I think my accent syncs back to that whenever I'm talking to a Scot. Where are you from up there?" I slip in to prevent further questioning; a tactic from my protection training: people love talking about themselves.

"Oh, I'm a highland girl born and bred. Right, I must get back to it," she says, a little abruptly. "You give me a shout if you need anything, OK? And make sure your wee heater is turned on before you drop off; we cross the border in the early hours and it gets bloody chilly on board."

"Will do, thanks, Isla," I say.

As she approaches my compartment door she sees my book lying open on the fold-down tray. It's just a trashy whodunit murder I bought from WH Smith back at the station and placed there as part of Clay's 'life litter'. The book has a sanderling feather I use as a bookmark resting on the page. She has her back to me so I can't see her face but for a second I'm sure she stopped dead in her tracks as if she'd seen something far more horrific than the crap Agatha Christie wannabe.

She regains herself and shuffles away down the corridor and I hear her burst into conversation with another passenger as if they're a long lost relative and it makes me feel a little resentful that her warmth isn't reserved just for me.

I like Isla, but I like who I am with people like her and that's more significant.

Subconsciously, we all hold a constant image of ourselves in our mind. It's like a little faded Polaroid and it changes depending on who we are with. For example, when I am in my manager's office in London the Polaroid in my mind depicts a withdrawn, furrow-browed Clay; when I am speaking to a shop assistant or receptionist the Polaroid evolves to a tall, well-dressed, superior Clay. The different images of myself change as easily as one of those hologram postcards you'd send from your holiday as a child; simply tilt me towards a different person and the image of myself morphs.

I wonder whether everyone has multiple selves in their minds or whether this is yet another by-product of living as a many-faced chameleon the way I do.

My legend training began in the spring of 1997. Constable Clark of Castlebay Police introduced my family to the Regional Commander of the Protected Person Unit, Scotland arm of the UK Protected Persons Service. I learned that the programme is part of the National Crime Agency (NCA) and comprises a team of former and current police officers with specialist skills. I understood that protection isn't only for those who are testifying in court, Goodfellas such as Henry Hill; the programme protects the vulnerable in general. That was what I had been designated: vulnerable.

I was assigned Programme Officer Bernadette Cruickshank (Bernie), who explained that the media reaction to Classroom B was the reason I required protection. It had been decided that any mention of my presence that day or any association with the event in general was to be avoided in order to preserve some form of normality in my future. However, that also robs you of any potential sympathy from the general public and in the years following Classroom B, many initiated hate campaigns against my mum and anyone from the area who shared the name Kinkade.

With such a small, tight-knit community Castlebay was like any other perfect environment for bacteria to grow; intimate, damp and dark. It was a foregone conclusion that I would have to be moved away and as I reached the minimum age threshold of twelve, Nana and Grandpa had fully endorsed my entrance onto the programme.

I asked Bernie whether Sorrell was going into the programme too but she said she couldn't talk about others and that I was her focus, which I revelled in.

Bernie explained that her job was a solution for vulnerable people like me, "Someone to help you start anew so that you can have the same opportunities that everyone else has." She outlined what generating and maintaining a new persona or "Legend" entailed. It was terrifying. Bernie reminded me of my Aunty Gill, solid and sympathetic in equal measure, sharp and capable. A cuddly soldier.

As my Programme Officer, Bernie was a plain-clothes policewoman but in all honesty I think many a criminal could spot her from a mile away, because Bernie didn't quite wear civilian plain clothes, she wore what she *thought* were civilian plain clothes. Blue, fitted, stonewash jeans, a white or grey T-shirt tucked into said jeans, covered by a weathered light brown leather jacket with those worn cracks in the material. She had a mane of curly hair that seemed to hit every colour from mousy brown to grey. This plain jane, nothing-going-on-here look was completed with a pair of overly large, overly bright, white Hi-Tec running trainers. As a result I don't think anyone would have been surprised to learn that the frayed stitches on her waistline above her right buttock pocket were not caused by a child or apron but was where her enormous police radio was holstered. That was Bernie. Bernie liked Van Morrison, playing him whenever we were in the car, and disliked people who wanted Scotland to become independent from the UK because she found the concept of a united kingdom of countries on a wee island very romantic.

Within days Bernie introduced me to her colleague Faisel Shepherd, who was from something called the Behavioural Science team, Faisel immediately requested I call him Fiz. It was his responsibility to help me build my new persona, ensuring it was both robust and versatile.

"The best lies are based on truth," he said at the

start of our first meeting. Bernie and Fiz deemed Uncle Gordon's cottage a perfect place for me to dissolve Castlebay and rebuild my personality from the ground up. "Comfortable enough to remain around family but secluded enough from Castlebay for his welfare to be secure," I overheard Bernie say to Fiz one afternoon.

It was March 1997. I hadn't seen mum for a couple of years at that point but I was kept occupied grappling with the daily regime.

We awoke early and after a short set of exercises and breakfast with Fiz, we got straight down to it, taking up numerous positions around the back living room while we trawled over my old life, contorting it into a new, stronger but altogether different life.

It was an astonishing operation, and after a few weeks Fiz briefed Nana and Grandpa to go out and do menial things to develop 'life litter'. These could be tickets, photographs, anecdotes, experiences or time stamps; anything to generate a footprint. It was exhausting but so novel for a young boy and a great distraction from the events that haunted me. I thought about Sorrell constantly and whenever I became subdued Fiz seemed to disappear from whichever room or corridor we were in and Bernie would silently appear.

Fiz taught me how to read people. "Thinking on your feet is super important in the future, OK pal?" He'd make me feel like I was playing a computer game. "OK, let's play. You're player 1, I'm 2. My

character is Dave, the schoolfriend; your character is Tom, cool?" We'd role play multiple times a day.
"So where're you from?"
"I'm from the rural region of Scotland," I'd respond.
"That's too formal, matey, it sounds rehearsed, you know? Answer like you normally would but just swap the words, Castlebay is Glen Coe, yeah?"
Fiz's advice was to use my own life up until that point, until my training began, as a fertile field on which to grow a new life: that way if your depths are probed you can reach for a root which is close by but not the real one. Day by day we rewound my life, razed it to the ground and rebuilt it from the rubble.
"Have you ever seen those archaeology shows on TV?" asked Fiz. "You know, when the presenter shows us those tiny walls? Like the footprint of someone's house with the small little crumbled foundations showing the outline of where a Roman kitchen or cow shed was? That's what we need: rooted foundations that give us a good start but we can update the building to take whatever shape we want."
I make this sound as if I could make myself into anyone I wanted. That's not true. I could flesh out the details of my new persona but I was given the starting points to which I must adhere as they had been preselected by the Protection Unit's analysis.
The problem faced by the Protection Unit was that major cities and conurbations tend to be

more connected with higher levels of varied media consumption and so they are seldom selected as appropriate places to hide a person. There are simply too many eyeballs.

I learned Castlebay was an especially unfortunate place to suffer a tragedy like Classroom B, because it's so distinctive. It's incredibly remote, picturesque and unique, with distinguishing features like Kisimul Castle. All of these elements become attached to the case, they become its connotations, and so similar locations were also deemed less than perfect for my relocation.

At fifteen I'd had enough of the training and pushed my handlers to allow me to move but they constantly countered that I wasn't ready yet. At night in bed I'd stare at the map Gordon had tacked to the wall – "Wonderful Walks of Great Britain" – and wonder which path I would take when I was finally released.

CHAPTER 17

Feasting in the Dining Car

S taring through the window as we fly through England like a maniacal flicker book, my eyes try to fix on the people I see, but the speed means I can only capture them as photographs like stills frozen in state. A fluorescent-jacketed worker lifting a fuse box. A deflated adolescent leaning over a textbook beneath a lamp in their terraced window. I feel a nervous energy pushing me to walk, although my heart rate still appears to be slow and steady.

I slide the narrow horizontal latch across on my compartment door and step into the cramped, slim corridor. It's draughty and smells like the scout huts that I played in as a boy, a blend of worn carpets and stale tea. The world still rushes past the window and I brace my steps with my arms on each side of the corridor as the carriage sways through Ordinaryville on the outskirts of

Forgottenland. I know what I'm searching for; the corridor does not offer it yet, but I can smell it.

Walking through the next carriage, my eyes guiltily wander upwards from beneath my brows in search of any life on which to pry. I come upon a large room the windows of which stretch along much of the corridor, packed with people in elaborate clothing. The women wear ballgowns and the men morning suits with long tails and formal hats. The indoor smoking ban came into force in the UK about 15 years ago so I'm shocked to see most of this group with cigarettes in hand. They stand in a crescent listening to one small man wearing a Homburg hat on top of slick black hair. He holds the lapels on his jacket as well as the attention of this group in his hands.

I slow my pace to try and catch what is being said. "Because, you see," exclaims this confident auteur in a Belgian accent, "if the man were an invention – a fabrication – how much easier… to make him disappear!" The crowd draws a collective gasp.

I keep moving slowly in order not to arouse suspicion but at the last minute the man turns his head slowly, revealing a petite handlebar moustache with peaks at either end and spectacles perched on the end of his nose. He smiles at me knowingly.

I continue down the corridor and the smell I'm tracking gets stronger. Walking through the corridor, finally some life: a young couple approach me in a playful embrace, giggling and nuzzling one another, until they arrive at their compartment and collapse through it to the sound of explosive laughter before the thin, plastic door is slammed for privacy.

At last I'm here. The motion sensor appears to be broken on this door and so I lift a small latch and as if spring-loaded the door shoots back into its frame, unleashing a completely new atmosphere. Noise, pouring, calling, munching, laughing, clinking and talking. The Restaurant Carriage, the watcher's feast.

I step forward to the sound of blaring 1920s trumpets where the bow-tied waiters appear to dance around each white-clothed table with tall, steaming, golden coffee pots. There's a sweet smell of strudel in the air mixed with the undeniable richness of truffle.

A delicate waiter with a pencil moustache approaches me and raises an inquisitive single finger, mouthing "just one?" I nod yes and he swivels on his heel and leads me to the orphan section, the single loner table positioned as an island in the middle of the carriage away from all of the surrounding double and quadruple, leather-studded booths on either side benefiting from the window views. You may take issue with this table but for me it's utterly perfect, as it places me in the middle of all of these ordinary people, whom I can watch.

I sit down at the small, square, clean-clothed table and the waiter uses his brio to whip the pages of his pad over to a fresh page "*Welcome*, sir" he purrs with evident pleasure. "My name is Arthur and I will be looking after you this evening. Are you with us all the way to the Highlands?" he enquires with the sincerity that a member of your family would use.

"I am actually, yes," I reply with a slight Irish lilt.

"First time?" he asks, implying he means the sleeper train as his eyeballs arc in their sockets at our surroundings.

"It is. I'm heading north for some hiking near Glen Coe."

This time his expressive eyes widen with excitement but with less sincerity as he doesn't strike me as a climbing type.

"How delightful," he oozes. "Such a wonderfully theatrical mode of transport to take you to your Scottish adventure; personally I always find the carriages rather cinematic!"

"Hmm," I respond, "I'm not really into films."

"Each to his own, sir... and with what can I tickle your fancy this evening?"

"Just a peach iced tea, thanks, and can you leave it in the bottle please?" I request. The waiter swivels once more, never seeming motionless, his ankle-length black apron twirling like a flamenco dancer, and heads to a semi-circular ornate art deco bar to my left where a pointed-eared barman with centre-parted lacquered hair stares back at me. The Polaroid of myself in my mind depicts a relaxed Clay in his natural habitat as sharp, sweet cocktail bitters cut through the air.

Straight ahead. Tall, suited, slim man of at least sixty years old but the leatheriness of his sun-battered skin is adding at least five years to him. His hair is thin but still present, grey but still shines, and is swept back over his dome-like head with a wet-look product. I'll call him Old Money. He wears a double-breasted cut pinstriped suit with wide lapels and a pinky ring adorns his little finger, advertising his taste for the traditional. He leafs through the *Financial Times* with a nonchalance that tells me he controls much of the news that he reads in its pages. His leather Church's Derby shoes are classic, pristinely clean but unlaced to relieve swelling; his job in the city is obviously taking its toll. Old Money is heading home to his country manor house which he inherited from his father and he will pass to his clone son. Old Money runs this country.

Over to my right are a couple aged in their mid to late fifties. Neither of them is over five foot four inches, and both of them wear the same colour and brand of anorak despite the lounge car's perfect temperature. He occasionally consults a long, slim trainspotting paperback book, lifting his chin and dropping his eyes downward through his reading spectacles. His full and stained moustache twitches like a dog about to sneeze as he enjoys whatever rail facts the book offers. He puts it down and stares straight ahead. His wife straightens a fork that was already straight and stares straight back over his shoulder. Mr and Mrs Monotone. The Monotones ran out of conversation fifteen years ago and each regrets their early retirement. Rain awaits them at every campsite they visit.

The waiter returns with my ice tea, placing it lightly on the table, rotating it so that the label faces me as if it is a bottle of £900 wine, then sliding it gently towards me. A champagne cork pops across the carriage and someone irritating unleashes an almighty guffaw. My annoyance is sidelined as another waiter whips past me carrying a hot platter beneath a dramatic silver cloche from which a seductive, creamy, cheesy, seafood smell trails.

At the table behind me on my right by the window, there is a pocket of silence; an empty table maybe? I turn to investigate and see a woman. Mid thirties in age she has short, plain, brown hair. She sits with the purposeful posture of someone attending a royal banquet. She's dressed practically with flat shoes and a thick, nondescript waist-length coat which is zipped up to her chest leaving just enough space to make out her deep blue nurse's uniform underneath and a National Health Service lanyard around her neck. She looks through the window with a focused stare as the scenery flashes by. I'm calling her Hushed Valour. Hushed Valour has just finished a thirteen-hour shift plugging wounds, holding hands and checking drips.

The train ploughs into another tunnel and the scenery outside vanishes, replaced by black brick walls, the lounge lights temporarily turning each window into a reflection. Hushed Valour notices me watching her and turns away from our reflections towards my table; her mouth offers the most delicate of smiles, which I return. Hushed Valour is there for us all.

The train has reached its metronome speed now, a steady 80 mph that will carry it through the heart of England. I look out of the window and the sun is starting to sink as we skirt around Coventry, I finish my iced tea and leaving my strudel untouched I get up to continue my wander.

As I inch my way through the dining area I see Mr Monotone has dropped his trainspotting book. I bend down and pick it up, feigning tying my shoelace. The lounge car door senses my approach and slides open, I walk through and slip the book into my pocket.

CHAPTER 18

Hell is a Sanctuary

T he fact that with every second I am speeding closer to my homeland aboard this train is making it increasingly difficult to silence the voice in my head that urges me to go back there, to that day in Castlebay. As I walk the carriages, the voice plagues my thinking and I realise I'm uncertain as to where on the train I am in relation to my cabin, but this doesn't stop my feet. I'm beginning to succumb. I'm not ready to go back to that day just yet, so my memories settle on the days that followed it, the closest they dare wander for now.

I was unaware of how much of a surrogate Nana and Grandpa had become in the weeks that followed 7th January in 1991. When they and Aunty Gill were increasingly required to attend the police station and meet with solicitors, I longed for them, even more so when I was smuggled to Uncle

Gordon's house on Hellisay, a tiny and largely uninhabited island just off the coast of Barra. Unbeknownst to me this is where I would live for the next ten years.

Uncle Gordon was a quiet man. Unambitious and kept to himself. I never felt Nana and Grandpa liked him. He'd come to Castlebay to help Mum fit the kitchen when we first moved in and had never left. He lived behind a small valley on Hellisay, a natural fortress. When I think back today, I often wonder if his house is still there, and if it is, the ridiculously high rate he could charge for it on Airbnb due to its spellbinding location. A cottage, nestling in the shadows of sheer hills either side; in my eyes it was the most secluded place on earth. That was Gordon. Gordon liked lemon curd on crumpets and overused the phrase "I'll give credit where credit is due" and he disliked social gatherings of any kind.

If you want to shield a child from a trauma that is engulfing their village and from a swarming pack of media, Gordon's cottage is possibly the most perfect place on earth. And so it was decided, "The little one would go and stay at Gordon's." I remember my family being so busy with Mum at the police station that a policeman was asked to go to The Craigard and pack me a bag for my time away from home. When I arrived at Uncle Gordon's and opened it up, I giggled at the contents and spent the next few weeks of winter dressed as if I were heading to the beaches of Spain.

Uncle Gordon had no children. He had no wife. Most of all, Gordon had no sociability. Conversation in the first two weeks was painful. Never had two human beings been thrust together with less to say to each other. Uncle Gordon's speech was like a marble rolling across a wooden floor then tumbling down three steps in quick succession only to roll for another mile. A sort of uncertain, continual, nondescript, elongated drone that then sparked into life and spawned two or three coherent words, only to abruptly die.

I longed to know what had become of Sorrell, where had she gone. Was she hiding on another Hebridean island like me? Had she been taken further away?

Eventually, both Gordon and I conceded, and without actually saying the words to each other we agreed that we no longer need to feel compelled to say *any* words to each other. And so began what was supposed to be six months at Uncle G's with nothing but a Ferguson VHS toploader video player and corded remote control to occupy my blank mind. In the first weeks movie upon movie filled the empty days, Hitchcocks, Spielbergs, spies, westerns, while I wondered what had happened to my regular life, to my friends and, most of all, to Sorrell.

It was six weeks before I saw Mum.

It was a dreary Sunday afternoon and I heard a rustling in the back garden. Startled, I scurried to the pantry to see what kind of animal had wandered down from the mountain to forage in Gordon's carrot patch only to see Grandpa emerge from the trees. It wasn't apparent to me then but he'd clambered through the back garden bushes to evade the media who had even hired boats to crawl around the islands off Barra.

Gordon would shrink when in the presence of Grandpa.

"They're letting her see him," muttered Grandpa, seemingly utterly demoralised and devoid of any energy.

"Righto, Pa, and how is she?" Uncle Gordon enquired.

"What do you think, lad?" he snapped. "Where is he? I need to be sharpish, we've only been given a wee slot… Come on, my old China!" Grandpa said in a warm tone after noticing me behind him "We'll go and see Ma."

I scampered around the corner towards the front door but Grandpa halted me, stroked the crown of my head with his enormous, leathery hand and manoeuvred me towards the back door. "Put this on, laddie," he said, handing me a large, dark green anorak that smelled of mould. "And pull that hood up, OK?"

We stepped out into the back garden and headed off into the trees. I was immediately confused because the road was in the opposite direction, at the front of Uncle Gordon's cottage, so where were we going? We walked for about 15 minutes in pure silence, the only sound the snap of twigs beneath Grandpa's old shoes and the occasional whisper of naked branches as the wind wafted through the bitter woods. Finally we arrived at Grandpa's ancient, faded Rover 200 and set off towards the ferry to Castlebay.

Grandpa hurriedly grabbed at the radio dial to switch it off and the warm air from the heater pounded my cheeks. "Chin up, laddie." We wound through the country lanes to the north of the valley, edging around the island hills.

Looking out of the window over the fields as we drove, the dreary skies looming over grassy hills, derelict barns and dry-stone walls stirred a vulnerability within me, while a faint voice inside tried to distract me, whispering "Straw Dogs". We passed Kerin's farm, where a sign had recently been erected on the top of an old concrete fence post. Grandpa grasped the back of my neck and squeezed, and my eyes snapped forward, concentrating on the tarmac through the windscreen. We continued through the hills. The makeshift signs became more frequent, Atop fence posts, hay bales or stiles, and finally Grandpa seemed to succumb and accept he could not prevent me from seeing them.

"Burn her" were the words I caught as we drove past the next sign. "Execution" was all I could make out from the one after that as Grandpa sped up.

The following months saw me make similar clandestine trips, to visit a doctor's office in Griminish on a larger island a little farther north called North Uist. Aged eight I was old enough to notice that trips to the doctors were coming at a far higher rate than had been the case before the events in Classroom B. But they stopped as I reached nine when the doctors seemingly decided I was coping.

The vitriol across the islands towards the Kinkade name only grew stronger in the subsequent months, however, and I withdrew more to my cave at my uncle's on Hellisay.

More solitary days ensued with more VHS movies stacked outside my door by Uncle Gordon. A lonely boy being supported by Marty McFly and Mick Dundee.

Gordon's chess friend Fergal Douglas was a retired island doctor. He would visit and sit silently for hours opposite my uncle pondering the board. I recall him finding me very interesting, as if the trauma I'd experienced made me some captive creature for him to study. He'd continually ask me quiz-like questions about how I viewed my life or myself.

"Do you often feel bored, my boy?"

"If you pushed me over and I banged my knee, would you feel bad?"

"Do you like talking to me?"

"What comes to mind when I say your mum's

name, Rhona Kinkade?"

"Who's the most important person in your life, lad?"

"We all tell porky pies in life; how many do you think you've told this week?"

I wasn't interested in Dr Fergal's quiz. I asked anyone who would listen about Sorrell's whereabouts. But I never got an answer. They had bigger concerns. Eventually I managed to cajole Grandpa into asking around and discovered that as soon as their statements had been submitted and the police had approved them to leave, Sorrell's parents had fled the Scottish Hebrides, completely grief-stricken.

"Plenty more fish in the sea, my old china," Grandpa repeatedly said in an attempt to cheer me up.

Soon after, as I approached eleven years old, Barra Constabulary submitted me for the Vulnerable Person Protection Programme.

CHAPTER 19

Polly for a Picture

The dining carriage has satisfied my hunger for the 'good stuff'. And I don't mean the strudel. Slipping my hands into my pockets and staring at my feet walking through another carriage I look down, take out the trainspotting book I stole from Mr Monotone and begin to feel strange, as I always do after taking something that isn't mine. I make that sound as if I'm some rabid kleptomaniac. I'm not; I only ever steal for a reason. Can I attribute the behaviour to some mutation from my protection programme training? Probably not. That taught me to hide, not steal. Although the two do go hand in hand and I lift a jacket hung outside someone's cabin as I'm always in need of new clothing without leaving a trail.

There's only ever been one occasion where I've stolen something for no apparent reason and ironically it's become the most crucial item I own.

I have numerous memories of being sat atop Barra's largest hill, Heaval summit, looking out over the bay while Sorrell explained to me how the collective term for seagulls was a "herd" or some other ridiculous musing.

It was around four months before the tragedy at school when Sorrell told me about a new adventure of which she'd become aware, Boyd's house, or boat to be more exact. On the west slope of Heaval the ground breaks into a basin and a collection of small streams feed a tiny loch named Uisge. It's at the northern lip of this loch that Boyd's houseboat was moored.

Boyd was Barra's warning story, the person parents would reference when trying to steer their children away from bad decisions. "All you need to do is look at Boyd, my love," my mum would say.

Boyd was the only child of Grant and Esme Erskine, Barra's most regal of families. The Erskines were tight-knit and wealthy. They weren't aristocratic with wealth, or, as Mum would say, "They weren't built-in with Barra's brickwork"; they'd acquired it through shrewd business acumen. They were a working-class family who suddenly found themselves with brass plug sockets and golden stair runners, things I thought represented real wealth when I was a boy. Despite ordinary beginnings, the Erskines became like Castlebay's answer to the Kennedys, waving modestly but majestically at the frequent applause. But instead of hundreds of thousands lining Capitol Hill, the Erskines had around twenty-eight sitting on church chairs sinking in the mud.

Their spoiled troll of a son, Boyd, remained. He'd gambled away the family fortune, which had resulted in Grant and Esme leaving Barra. The shamed prince moved to a houseboat and that's where Sorrell was leading me on that drizzly September morning.

"I know when he goes out," she boasted, her wild hair looking even more untamed, now damp from the drizzle. "He goes down to the surgery every Wednesday to collect his medicine, my mum told me!" she whispered salaciously.

We slowed our steps as the track wound tighter and deeper towards Loch Uisge. Stepping closer to the houseboat, we were surrounded by lush, moist greenery, which filled our nostrils with smells of cow parsley and congealing mud while fat raindrops pattered off the leaves.

Even without prior knowledge of this surprise adventure I was still the more appropriately dressed of us with a purple mac and sturdy trainers. Sorrell on the other hand wore leather moccasins and a pair of denim dungarees over bare shoulders which stirred new levels of infatuation in me.

As we arrived at the edge of the tree line, my heart began to pump slightly faster and I realised I'd never been down to the water's edge, certainly not without Mum. My trainers squelched as the grass became a weedy marsh. I was hoping to spy Boyd leaving his houseboat, perhaps even being handed a pair of miniature binoculars by Sorrell to complete my Goonies fantasy, but it was not to be. She crouched beside me, brushing mud specks from her drenched shoulders and said, "He's out; shall we have a peek inside?"

The houseboat was located on the shoreline of the loch closest to Castlebay and I immediately recognised the public footpath which connected you to the village, yet we had taken a weaving hike all the way over Heaval summit. A smile dimpled my cheeks as I realised that ramble was Sorrell's attempt to hide the fact that Boyd's "mysterious and secluded" houseboat was actually a three-minute walk from our homes.

It stank. We'd entered through a cracked and warped plastic-framed back door. A simply built house with horizontal wood panelling and decking around the entire circumference, It was the caravan of the water. Sorrell's confident leadership had faded after she'd been startled by an unexpected hanging basket and she'd retreated to a more strategic position, peering from behind my shoulder.

The house was horrid. An accumulation of "I'll sort that later's". Dirty dishes, piles of mail, wires running across open flooring, loose panels, balled-up clothes, a truly haphazard home, a youngster's trove.

We began tentatively, respectfully. Leafing through papers as if perusing expensive items you know you can't afford in a shop, with raised eyebrows and upturned mouth, politely impressed by the offering. We quickly realised there was no need to stand on ceremony and the light-hearted ransacking began. Sorrell was immediately absorbed by Boyd's photograph albums, a rare look into the lives of the 'Barra Kennedys', but I was hunting for something specific, I had no idea what but I wanted it. It certainly wasn't the antique watch I remember grasping, or the wax stamp, or the bright varnished fishing floats, items that rushed through my fingertips as I scrambled over every surface, through every drawer and then…
Nothing.
I didn't happen upon the unnamed relic that I'd imagined, I didn't throw open a chest revealing a golden light. There was nothing I wanted to steal. I felt deflated. Sorrell had settled on a stool and was buried in the Erskines' pictorial family history. Too many films, I thought to myself; there's nothing here. I wandered to the deck and looked back inside; the place didn't look too dissimilar to when we arrived despite the frenzied search. I muttered to Sorrell that I wanted to go to the cafe in the bay for something to eat. I watched her silently nod, still engrossed in the huge A2 binder, then she placed it neatly back on the shelf but not before carefully peeling back the cellophane of a particular page, removing a Polaroid and slipping

it in her back pocket.

I was jealous. I wanted something of meaning. A treasure, an artefact, something to show off later. So as Sorrell trudged past me, I quietly dug my hand into an old fishing crate and pulled out the first thing I felt. Disappointingly it was a filthy old bottle of whisky.

Sorrell treasured the photo of the Erskines. Whether it was the feeling of local history, or the realness from knowing some of the people in the photo, she loved it and would keep it on her whenever we went on adventures.

It didn't take long for me to covet the photo and over the subsequent weeks I remember cajoling her to swap it with the bottle of booze I'd taken. And so after two months of persuasion Sorrell agreed to give me the faded picture of the Erskine family in exchange for a bottle of golden liquid which had a picture of a ship on the label named SS *Polly*.

Days later I discarded the photo. It had lost its shine since I'd acquired it. And I've often regretted not keeping that old bottle of SS *Polly* when I discovered its value a few years ago.

CHAPTER 20

Bad and Ugly

My wandering continues, and for some reason I feel the need to walk to the train's extremity in the hope there's an observation car to view the scenery. It will also help me keep my mind from going to Classroom B. The memories of it have been scuttling about my head since boarding but I'm surprised to see the exercise tracker on my wrist shows a steady, almost lethargic heart rate of 42. The corridors are filled with that white noise that comes from high-speed travel, a broad but dull roar of wind that never stops.

I pause at various windows during my walk and savour the sensation of being whisked through the landscape. It makes me realise I'm actually looking forward to being back in my homeland of Scotland. Most people likely feel propelled by a train, being pushed along the tracks forwards, but

I'm overcome by a feeling that the train is being pulled across the British Isles, as if some huge magnet sits up there in the Highlands and I'm finally giving in to its draw, meandering through the towns and fields in an increasingly excited trance.

"You're the only passenger I've seen stare longingly at Birmingham, my lovely," exclaims Isla behind me. I turn to pull focus and she looks somehow bashful and young, almost childlike.

"Ever get the feeling you've been somewhere before but not as a kid or something, but in another life? That sounds weird, I bet, I just mean another version of you was there…"

I become aware that I'm leaving interestingly abstract man territory and encroaching on batty abstract man, so I rein it back, but as I'm trying to justify my mindless chatter she interrupts me.

"I know exactly what you mean, like you're peering into another universe and once upon a time a version of you was wandering around in it, living a version of life there…"

As she says this she holds my gaze, her eyes looking longingly at mine as if she's been carrying her innermost thoughts in a locked box all her life, searching for people to unlock it and my key just clicked it open.

"Great minds think alike," I say lightly, trying to bring us both back from the gooey, dreamlike state of staring.

"I'm…"

"Clay," she finishes the sentence for me. "Yes, I remember, compartment 23, English Breakfast tea, no milk," she smiles.

A small buzzer sounds overhead and an 'assistance needed' light flashes on the wall signalling that a passenger has maybe fallen over in the toilets or had some other minor accident. Her sense of duty crashes over her sweet face and she snaps back into professional mode, making her excuses and leaving swiftly.

I hate to see you go, but I love to watch you leave, I think to myself.

I turn my attention back to the window to see the dark Victorian view of industrial Birmingham in the distance. It's dystopian and haunting and Rufus Sewell is running from strangers along the rooftops.

I continue walking the carriages and thinking of the bottle of SS *Polly* I swapped with Sorrell. It's the only link between us. Like the powerful blend described on its label, it's the thing that blends Sorrell and me, that blends Castlebay and me.

I'm distracted by a noise. At first I cannot make out its source amid the gush of wind and chatter of wheels on the track but I stop walking to concentrate. It's a fast, rhythmic drumming noise: bad-ah-bur, bad-ah-bur, bad-ah-bur. My eyes are scanning while my head swivels, searching for the cause of this foreign sound when I am suddenly frightened by the high-pitched whinny of a horse at full speed. I turn to the window aghast and can make out the silhouette of a pack of horses galloping noisily alongside our speeding train, ridden by a menacing posse of men in hats. They snarl and growl, thrashing the beasts to maintain speed, all the while pointing aggressively to the window where I'm standing. Then, without warning or preparation, one of them seems to be climbing out of his saddle and BANG! He must be on board. I'm terrified. Bodiless footsteps stomp closer but I know not from where. Thick heels on metal; is he on the damn roof!? They're heavy and booted. As the steps draw nearer they're accompanied by a grisly cackle, the owner clearly gleeful at my terror. The speaker system on the ceiling plays a folkish harmonica tune that causes my muscles to spasm.

I've cowered backwards into a corner in the carriage by now, frantically staring at all openings over and over, scared to take my eyes off any one of them in case this outlaw comes crashing through it. Sweat rolls down my nose and my fingernails bite into the carpet.

Then a hot breath reeking of bourbon and chewing tobacco is at my shoulder and I can feel coarse stubble graze my neck.

"Boo!" says a grisly voice.

I scream and turn sharply to see the man, his face still beneath the shadow of a large Stetson, but I can make out a mangled mouth with few teeth and a long wispy moustache draped over disfigured lips. Before I can do anything he grasps a handful of hair at the back of my head.

"Well, a lucky here, I think I found me a bounty!" he whispers like some unearthly animal. Then, with no warning, he jabs the corroded barrel of his revolver under my chin. I hear the unmistakable crank as he pulls back the pistol's iron hammer. I grit my teeth and long for that renowned flicker book of life to unfold rapidly on the insides of my eyelids.

Click. The man erupts into laughter.

"Listen, boy, the bounty on you says yous gots to be alive and a kicking." He licks his lips and rubs his palm over his crotch. "So I'd be a horse's ass to shootcha".

I feel dizzy and nauseous.

"Where you trying to get to?" the man asks.

"What?" I respond, still in shock.

His tone changes. "I said, to where are you heading this evening, sir?"

Sir? I think to myself and press my palms against my eyes.

"We're just leaving Birmingham, sir; may I check where you're headed this evening?"

I whip my hands from my face to see a short, rotund ticket inspector, his small, neatly trimmed moustache twitching with concern.

"Might I check your ticket, sir?"

He thinks you're a stray who's wandered on board, I think to myself.

"I'm sorry, I er–" I fumble my ticket in his face continually apologising while wiping the sweat from my neck and nose before sheepishly but hastily slipping back to my carriage. All the while that ominous country-style harmonica wails at me from the speakers.

CHAPTER 21

Tormenters

My head feels fogged. I'm walking the corridors trying to clear it when I happen upon the observation carriage. The roof is beautifully convex, bulging outward towards the sky and providing huge panoramic views of the landscape shooting by. The dark is drawing in now as we approach the industrial town of Crewe in Cheshire, north-west England.

In the carriage I find three fellow passengers, all women. They sit around a moon-shaped table in a booth, their faces lit from low golden lampshades nestled amid their salubrious cocktails.

One isn't saying anything; she's draped herself in a superior, arrogant slouch, staring away from the other two.

The freckled redhead in the middle seems high on something, her eyes bulging while she gesticulates and twitches.

The last one, clearly the youngest, is gentle and mouselike. She's talking too but seemingly not in conversation with the other two, she just chatters silently to herself.

The box-mounted wall speakers play muffled 1920s band music and the white-jacketed barman rotates a cloth inside a glass to dry it while looking at me sporadically. "Your money's no good here, Mr Torrance, orders from the house," I hear, but no one's mouth is moving. All work and no play makes Clay a dull boy.

"I'll have Three Feathers whisky, double, no ice," I say to the barman and drink it down quickly as soon as it arrives. Behind him is a vast wall of ornate liquor bottles on glass shelves in front of a huge mirror, the silver of which is fading at the corners.

The observation carriage is the last in the line and so walking to the back window I can see the track stretch out behind us. I lean against the window for a moment and just watch. The relentless flashing of tracks hypnotises me and my mind snatches at memories of Classroom B, of that darkest of days on 7th January. A shake of the head and they vanish with a sizzle like a hot match dropped into water.

My shoulders slump into the salubrious wingback Chesterfield armchair when the carriage door clatters open and the Caledonian Sleeper's busiest trolley dolly sweeps through.

"Well, hello, my lovely; interest you in a little

snifter?"

"A what?" I feign confusion. I know exactly what she's referring to but haven't heard a short alcoholic evening drink referred to as that in the years since I left Scotland.

"A nightcap; you've a whole back bar to choose from."

"Ah, no thanks Isla, I'm not really a drinker," I lie.

"Suit yourself. Enjoying the journey?" she enquiries, wiping literally everything she passes with a very sad and tired cloth.

"I am, now that you're here," I respond playfully, which brings a short, surprised giggle from her.

"Time for a coffee break yourself? I could use the company."

We chat a while and I feast on the good stuff.

This is Isla. Isla likes to bake and finds disabled people who are seemingly alone very upsetting, to the extent she once stayed on a bus for twelve stops to ensure a young man with Down syndrome was not lost.

Isla idolises the emergency services, finding even the smallest actions of paramedics very moving.

Isla loves to sketch and attempts to limit this to bedtime, just after brushing her teeth and just before dropping off to sleep. Regardless of what she plans to draw, her hand always settles on a tiny figure. A child. Some of these sketches have broken out of their designated time in her daily life and litter the paper on which her refreshment orders are written. This miniature character is scattered across her papers and I long to ask who it is and why she never finishes its face.

She talks of various passengers she's met over the years and I'm struck by how she often studies the role of chance, fate and serendipity in life. For some reason this irks me to the point of anger and I have to try hard not to snap at her: we control our own life, it isn't some map predetermined by the "divine".

She seems genuinely happy but sporadically her mask slips and behind it sits pain, and I long to ask her to tell me all about it. Does that make me caring or morbid, I wonder.

Despite the stained tea towel stuffed into her waistband, chipped nail varnish and utterly wild black hair she's strikingly beautiful and I'm taken by the feeling I want her to stay and talk until we arrive at our destination but I know she can't. Within minutes she's up on her feet and backing away, making her apologies while buffing the bronze lamp at the same time.

"I'm sure I'll see you again before Fort William," I say as she strides to the door, at which she turns around and smiles as if she's ten years old.

The lights have dimmed now, as if they're losing power, and the carriage feels drunk and lazy.

I'm just about to leave when a young man appears at the bar of the observation car looking to order a drink. "I think they've closed up for the night," I say, arching forward slightly and tilting my head to get a better view of my new carriagemate.

Still facing away from me he nods silently, seeming slightly disappointed.

"You sailing the rails all the way north?" I enquire of the back of his head.

He nods silently and I notice he's clutching something beneath his left arm.

"Yes... me too," I say nonchalantly, trying to set the guy at ease so I can get a closer look at what he's carrying, as he still hasn't turned to face me. He's definitely younger but he's keeping a flat train driver's cap tilted down and so I'm struggling to make out more. His posture is naive, vulnerable. As I creep closer, craning to see more, still muttering something about the train staff clocking off too early for proper drinkers like us, I steal I glance at the object in his hands. It's a model train and he has feathers scattered around his feet. Just then a signal bell rings loudly as we speed by and the noise makes me turn sharply to the window. When I return my eyes to the bar it is empty, the man has gone, there are no ladies in the booth and no feathers at my feet.

Unnerved, I return to the armchair and my head pivots like a pigeon over my shoulders; the distant laughter of children is back again but the carriage is empty.

It was only a matter of time before I gave in on this journey and let the memories of the day – from which I have been hiding – ooze back into my brain.

Classroom B.

My feet take me to the rear window where the tracks continually churn out behind us; we're climbing a steep mountainside and I have to lean backwards to steady myself. For the first time on the journey I want to get off this train. To let the incline take my weight and just tumble off so that I'm no longer chugging my way back to that island. It's the height of summer, a humid and breathless evening but from the corner of the window, spider-like legs of ice begin to form across the dark glass.

CHAPTER 22

Classroom B

7th January 1991: Scotland's Darkest Day

I remember being happy that day. Excited.

A right of passage when starting at Castlebay Primary is your self-portrait, when you are initiated as a Sanderling (named after a native beach bird of the island) by making your image with finger paints and decorating it with actual sanderling feathers. As Jack had started that year he was making his, and everyone was going to join in, including my friend, his sister Sorrell.

My memories are scratchy but I remember being in the toilets looking in the mirror and I was excited. I was in costume, wearing my feathers, and I was smiling from ear to ear.

Then I remember Classroom B being locked and the teaching assistant Miss Monroe asking what was wrong and me telling her that "the other four have said they're the flock but I'm not in it because I'm the teacher's kid." I'd turned the doorknob and it was locked, I'd told her.

Then I remember Miss Monroe took my hand and I hopped off the bench to walk alongside her, the poor wounded little boy whom she must reintegrate with these cruel little children.

I can see that moment so clearly in my mind. Her grip loosened and my hand fell to my side as she lunged for the door handle.

"Oh good *god!*" her voice said in a tone the depth of which I had never heard her use. The world 'god' was at a deafening volume which made me jump.

I stared at her. She covered her mouth and shook the door in its frame. "R-RHONA!?" She screamed for my mother. "WHERE'S THE – WHY IS IT? – RHONA!" She shrieked in demented desperation. She wasn't forming sentences, her voice an explosion of mangled syllables, and I stepped back instinctively as her body flailed against the door.

She turned and ran towards the assembly hall. I walked quickly behind her, her voice piercing my ears.

She ran across the hall where my mum was crouched, speaking on the telephone. The handset dropped from her hand with fright as she turned to focus on her teaching assistant sprinting toward her as if the ground behind her was falling away into a thousand foot canyon, shrieking, "THEY'RE DEAD!"

Everyone in the country knew about Scotland's Darkest Day. Probably many people in other countries too.

In 1991, four children were found hanging in Castlebay Primary's Classroom B. It shot through the British Isles like a convulsion. It is a story unparalleled in scale and infamy, and even terrorist attacks, as gory and horrific as they are, somehow pale beside this quiet, indescribable event when four tiny lives were seemingly taken by the very bodies they inhabited.

Months of inquest and investigations were conducted with the class teacher, my mother Rhona Kinkade, being held ultimately responsible for the tragedy that had happened in the tiny town.

Everything I knew before that day changed forever.

CHAPTER 23

The Mask is Slipping

The train is leaving Carlisle and finally crossing the border into Scotland. As it does I feel my stomach grow hot. I check my exercise tracker and my heartbeat hasn't moved. I walk tentatively back along the corridor to my cabin feeling the effects of the punchy whisky rolling through my bloodstream. I want to be alone as we breach the border.

Sitting hunched on my uncomfortable little fold-down chair I stare out of the window as my homeland comes into view. The trees take on the spiked silhouette of pines against the oceanic blue night sky. My hand creeps to my phone and searches again for Scotland's Darkest Day on YouTube, and the grainy 1990s newsreader footage pops onto the screen.

"This afternoon, schoolteacher Mrs Rhona Kinkade is being remanded in custody on gross negligence resulting in the deaths of four children in Castlebay on the Scottish Hebridean island of Barra. When asked if he was pleased with the result for the parents of the children, prosecution barrister Tony Trevelyon QC told the press: 'I'm not sure there will be any pleasure in the lives of anyone associated with this case for many years, indeed in the British Isles as a whole. We are broken.'"

The mention of Castlebay makes my stomach crackle and fizz once more.

I click my phone's lock button and the newsreader's face vanishes into the black screen. Pressing the phone against my mouth, my eyes well and escape to the view rushing past the window.

My jaw tightens and I feel tears run down my face.

But as my eyes let go of the scenery and focus on my reflection in the window, I'm surprised to see that I'm grinning broadly.

I don't know why I do that.

While the vistas have most definitely become more Scottish I feel like I can also smell my homeland. It's crisp and fresh and I'm gorging myself on it.

Strangely, despite it being summertime the temperature has dropped severely, as if nature can sense my presence and has ushered the warmth away. At this point nothing can keep my mind from that day. Not people-watching. Not drinking.

I have to let my mind go there.

As I watch Scotland fill the windows my breath begins to mist when I exhale.

How strange, I think to myself, as Father Lankester appears at my side clutching a crucifix while *Tubular Bells* plays over the ceiling speaker.

CHAPTER 24

Four Souls

T wo days after, on 9th January back in 1991, the charade unravelled like an old jumper. But such an innocent analogy is probably not appropriate for such a day. What I should say is that their charade unrivalled like an old jumper only to reveal a rotting, tarantula-infested nightmare beneath. I was sitting in the playroom applying the final ooze of glue to one of the numerous Airfix models that Grandpa had stacked in the corner. It was dusk, that point in the twilight hour where the sun succumbs to the horizon but its dying glow still soaks the room in a low, colder light. It's too dim to be daytime and too light to be night, the light is almost silver, it doesn't last long. I always felt vulnerable at that time of the day. Like the sun had been cloaking me from something, and now that it was slipping away I was bare, exposed to some faceless power that would inflict pain upon me.

Before I could uncross my legs to make for a soothing source of light via the switch high on the wall, the room lit up with a blinding flash. Perhaps only for a hundredth of a second, but it engulfed the room. My heart stopped. A second later there it was again. The most startling aspect of this light was its colour. It was an electric blue. I think most humans in the world immediately understand this light when it occurs, but for children a blue flashing light generally means one thing: danger. The siren was not sounding but the light was revolving as I nervously climbed to my feet. My mind locked my leg muscles like an early frost. "Where do I go?" I thought. "To Grandpa in the living room? To the front door to greet these scary people of authority."

I decided to go for the front door. I wandered into the hallway and felt my bare legs become warm. As if some invisible element was breathing on them, an almost hot sensation all around my thighs.

At that point Grandpa walked past me, towering overhead, and opened the door. "Good evening, officer," he said, at which point I looked down and realised I was wetting myself.

Scratchy voices babbled over the policeman's radio and he tilted his head towards where it was mounted on his shoulder to hear the message.

"Hello, sir," he said in a broad Barra accent. "The station phoned ahead to let you know we'd be coming, yes? I'm Constable Clark."

"Oh aye," replied Grandpa, putting his hand on the crown of my head to manoeuvre me out the way of the door as he heaved it open.

After Nana had addressed my stained shorts I was once again relegated to the dining room while the adults congregated in the kitchen. I bent my ear to the keyhole once more, searching for that cold blade of air that would rush through it, signifying my connection to the serious, adult world on the other side.

"Right, Mr and Mrs Kinkade, firstly I want to thank you for your cooperation in the last couple of days. We appreciate that this will be an immensely stressful time, so please do bear with us."

I remember thinking over and over: this sounds so serious.

"Let me also say that you should prepare yourself for quite a media assault on the village over the coming weeks or even months and that the Castlebay constabulary will look to support you wherever possible if and when this becomes overwhelming or intrusive.

"I have come here tonight as promised to give you an update on your daughter Rhona Kinkade. Ian, are you happy for Bee to hear this?"

The use of my Nana's shortened name told me this officer knew my grandparents well and explained why there was a slight tension in his voice.

"Aye, we both need to know, so can you just tell us? It's been bloody hell the last two days."

"All I can give you is the facts just now, and I would

strongly urge you not to discuss the case with anyone else until we advise you further."

"Aye, come on man, out with it!"

"Ian, it's looking like all four are gone."

At that point my Nana Beatrice yelped a horrifying scream that lasted for what felt like minutes. Usually, this was the point that a weathered and stern voice would awaken to comfort and guide Nana out of her upset, as I'd heard Grandpa do so often. But it did not come. I could hear no sounds of "Now come on, Bee, come on old girl, that's enough." Just shrieking. Shrieking which morphed to pitiful wailing and shot sharply back to shrieking as Nana rocked back and forth, clinging to her own body.

The policeman grappled to contain my Nana's eruption. It only subsided after around fifteen minutes when her body simply collapsed from the exhaustion of this thunderous emotion.

I opened the door slightly. Grandpa was down on one knee holding Nana next to the kitchen table while the policeman sat awkwardly at a professional distance on the other side. As the door creaked, Grandpa lifted his head wearily and sent me a look that said, "I cannot begin to imagine how to deal with this and you coming into the room is the least of my worries."

Strangely, Grandpa sinking his head back down to focus on Nana and not berating me for disobeying him was the most sobering moment of that evening. I froze in the crack of the doorway and watched.

"Where is she!? Where is she...?" Nana moaned from her exhausted tiny frame.

"She's at the station, Bee, she's down there with... they're looking after her."

At the age of five I was severely ill-equipped to process the discussion which then followed, and many would argue I should not have been privy to it at all. I stood helplessly by the dining room door and listened as the policeman gently rotated the volume setting on his shoulder radio to an almost silent level.

Then, as if reading from a script, he "regretfully informed" my grandparents that on Monday 7th January, their daughter, Rhona Kinkade, was alerted at eleven o'clock in the morning by me – their grandson – and teaching assistant Elsie Monroe that the door to Classroom B's "Little Sanderlings" was locked. Upon gaining entry a little after two o'clock, Miss Monroe found her class of four children – Kerin, Simone, Bobo and Jack – hanging from the main beam running down the north side of the room.

The days that followed played out almost exactly how that policeman had warned. The Craigard, our little secluded cove, carved from the island earth, became a circus. News vans parked haphazardly all over the road, each attempting to edge closer to the spectacle whenever someone moved.

While being cared for by my family in those dark

days all I could think about was Sorrell. She had not been there that day and so the news crews were all wrong. I was not the only survivor; there were two of us.

I barely watch the news nowadays. I don't like the intrusiveness of it all. Always focusing their lenses on someone.

It's approaching one o'clock in the morning on the train and the journey is taking its toll. But I find it cathartic to embrace my past and gallop towards it instead of constantly ducking and running from it.

I glance at my exercise tracker and my heartbeat still hasn't changed.

CHAPTER 25

Disdain

W e're slowing through Glasgow, one of the line's main stops and the first in Scotland. An announcement comes over the onboard speakers that there's a back-up of trains waiting to get into their respective platforms and so we'll be held for a short time.

As the train comes to a halt I can see the last of Glasgow's nightlife crawling onto the platforms intoxicated from the night's revelry and my mind pounces on them as an escape from thoughts of Castlebay.

Gawping, open-mouth breathing, sat on a platform bench. Looks South American from her colouring, jet black hair and mocha skin. Downward-turned facial features. Perpetually gurning. Short. Fat. Oversized Minnie Mouse T-shirt, circa 1997. Sat with legs open to accommodate her rotund gut. This is Brainless

Heifer. Heifer's view on life is like that of her namesake. She is bred, she looks for food, she is directed where to go and what to do, she feeds, she breeds, she dies.

Further up the platform my eyes rapidly scan and find a young man. Shrinking Violet we'll call him. He's the one person on that platform whom every single person has noticed. Tall, lanky, skinny, Muslim boy of about sixteen. His gaunt, nervous face has sprouted a full and impressive beard. He wears a salwar kameez, the long white, ankle-length tunic, oversized, hand-me-down K-Swiss trainers that are so large he's had to pull the laces as tight as possible resulting in the misshapen canoe look. His eyes dart up from beneath his hairy brow once every seven seconds searching for where the next sceptical look is coming from. He clutches a small man bag that is favoured among his cohort and is hitched high up on his body, resting against his chest. I feel like opening the window and announcing, "I don't think that's big enough for any kind of substantial improvised explosive so shall we all just stare at something else!?"

Eastern European jostling from my right entering the platform gates. Late thirties, bricklayer with the skin and hair of a sixty-year-old thanks to relentless chain smoking and high-strength lager. This is Rusted Cog. Rusted Cog wears unseasonably thick clothing, a base layer, sweater and a fleece jacket, with torn work trousers, everything caked in brick dust. Heavily scarred and tattooed hands with swelling fingers like rotten cigars. Eyes are shifty and slit-like, scanning the platform; the jovial and almost mischievous exchanges with his friend that follow make me feel they are sharing a joke, one about me. On the surface Rusted Cog looks brazen and confident but underneath he's simply glad to be away from the airstrikes and danger of his home country.

A girl arrives on the platform after waving to her friends. About seventeen years old, dressed provocatively, she struts confidently to the empty seat oblivious to the fact that an old, unsteady man was tentatively making his way to it from the other entry gate. No one says anything. This is Putrid Flower. Putrid Flower immediately opens her phone's camera and uses it to stare deeply at her face, adjusting her hair and rolling her lips. Despite appearing lost in her own world her eyes sporadically flit upward to check that, yes, people are in fact looking at her. Putrid doesn't need food or water to live, she needs eyes.

Travis Bickle is back at my shoulder. "Someday a real rain will come and wash this scum off the streets."

Leaning against the waiting room is a dishevelled mum lugging two suitcases with her four children in tow. For a second my eyes see Jack, Bobo, Simone and Kerin and I almost vomit.

The train engines groan and we clunk into motion with our sights set on the Highlands.

CHAPTER 26

Sick Humanoid

I'm standing outside my cabin, staring as we arc around Dumbarton. Thinking of my schoolfriends has mixed up my innards. It's a soup of melancholy, nostalgia and abject terror.

Then, there's a man approaching me from my left. He's tall, whitish pale and gaunt. He's dressed in an ill-fitting suit and his eyes appear glazed. I can't muster the enthusiasm for a hello and so I offer the quick raise of the chin, the laziest of greetings. He stops and stares over my shoulder. He's not looking at me but he's facing me and there's no one and nothing else in the corridor.

"Erm, hi?" I offer with a tone that expects an explanation. "You alright?" I ask.

He begins talking but there is no sound. His mouth is enunciating fluently but he is silent.

"Look," I say, growing more irritated and unnerved by this man. "I think you've had one too many." I give him a friendly pat on the upper arm, and it's as if I've pressed his unmute button, his sound is restored and his lengthy chattering finally has a voice.

"… when the tragedy occurred at the beginning of last year in the Scottish village of Castlebay when four children lost their lives." His voice is formal, stilted, almost scripted.

"'It's an event that continues to grip the nation,' said Prime Minister John Major earlier today while visiting Brussels. An inquest heard that Rhona Kinkade, the teacher convicted of gross negligence leading to the deaths, will be sentenced later this month."

I'm frozen to the core at the mention of Castlebay. The man is still not looking at me, and if I couldn't see the flesh on his face moving or smell his cheap 1990s aftershave I would be convinced he's some kind of sick humanoid robot. I try to engage him in conversation but he just continues, like a pre-recorded tape, sent out to chirp this horrible story.

"… the families of the children have formed a group and are lobbying the Government to improve the checks and monitoring of all employed education workers. A memorial garden is scheduled to open later this year in Edinburgh Castle in memory of the four children who died; Kerin Peacock, Simone Stott, Isobel Winkle and Jack Hutch."

I'm speechless. Angry that this freak won't actually look me in the eye but more terrified that another human being is saying this to me, to the survivor.

I inch away and he just stands there, awkwardly close to the corridor wall, straightening his tie and rearranging the script papers in his hand. His eyes are transfixed, gazing eerily into nothing, like a character in a video game unable to free itself from a glitch.

CHAPTER 27

Sorrell

The train is skirting the vast Loch Lomond. We can't be more than fifty miles from Oban on the west coast where my ferry docked that day when I was fifteen and my life began in earnest. This is the first time I've been back since. It feels strange. I feel as if I've lived twelve lives since leaving not just one.

And in a way I have.

I was the pot washer in a pub in Glen Coe.

The pickpocket on the buses of south Dundee.

The prostitute in Donnyglun council estate in Glasgow.

The holiday cabin cleaner in the Lake District.

The telemarketer selling kitchens in Hull, Yorkshire.

The night class history student in Bath, Somerset.

The deckhand on a trawler in Devon.

The hospital porter at the Royal London in Whitechapel.

The office assistant at an advertising agency in Farringdon.

The waiter at a Japanese/Jewish fusion restaurant in Belgravia.

The maître d' at a French brasserie on the South Bank.

And now the concierge at the Corinthia Hotel near Embankment.

Among all of these lives, there was one constant. I longed for Sorrell. I desperately wanted to talk to her about that day, to share my feelings and to hear hers.

I role-played conversations with her in my head, asking her why she had not attended school that day. Where did she go after leaving Barra so abruptly? Had she married? How had her parents taken Jack's death? Was she having to run and hide too? Did she have any questions for me? Did she want to know how that day impacted me? Did she think about me?

It became overwhelming.

And so, two years ago, while standing at the front desk in my job as assistant concierge at the Corinthia, one of London's finest hotels, I decided enough was enough. I had to find her. I would not compromise my legend, I'd invested too much in starting my new lives, but I would do what I could to find her. If I actually succeeded, what I'd do with the information was a whole other matter.

CHAPTER 28

A Fortuitous Trade

Two years ago I started thinking of ways to find Sorrell. I scoured my mind for things that could aid me, but the only connection was that old bottle of whisky that we'd taken from Boyd's houseboat. If I'd heard of its value then surely she would have too, which made me wonder whether she'd be tempted to do what I would have definitely done. Sell it! I had the idea to set up an online alert for any items connected to the SS Polly which were being sold, auctioned or even searched for. Thankfully the SS Polly and the load it shed is a fairly distinctive story and so I could be sure any alerts I received were going to be promising. But there were none. Two years I waited. And I ended up even forgetting about the alerts while I devised other ways to find out about the journey she'd taken since Castlebay.

I'd all but forgotten about that aspect of my hunt

for Sorrell when an email arrived in my inbox two weeks ago.

RARE! A unique treat for whisky enthusiasts: Bottle of 1943 SS Polly goes up for auction.

I frantically clicked the link and found it was a news story on the London *Evening Standard* website. A bottle was to be sold at auction at Sotheby's by a private seller this month. The article gave a brief synopsis of the ship's fate and the resulting handful of bottles that were squirrelled away by wily locals on the coast of a faraway Scottish island named Barra. It was actually a shock to read of my homeland in the press without mention of Scotland's Darkest Day for once, and in honesty it irked me. Within seconds I'd opened up a new browser window and was scrolling Sotheby's upcoming events. I found the bottle under February's "Gems of Our Isles" exhibition. Clicking faster still now I drilled further and further into the item details, feeling as if I was falling into the screen. Click, scroll, click, click.

And then I found it, the words I'd dreaded.

"Seller: anonymous".

That week I became morose. Skulking around my flat plotting ways to unmask the seller. It didn't take long for me to realise the answer lay at my place of work.

My job as a hotel concierge is a pseudonym for "fixer". The core attribute of any good concierge is to navigate seemingly insurmountable obstacles to make stuff happen. I've been a concierge at the Corinthia for four years, which is more than enough to have built a network of incredibly useful people. When I say useful I'm not talking about Hollywood stuff like retired police officers or autistic savant gamblers; my people are far more ordinary, but power can lurk in unlikely places. A night-time cleaner at Morgan Stanley. An intern at the *Times* newspaper. Chauffeurs to the children of politicians.

... and purveyors of the unique and sought-after, like Solomon Jacks.

Last week I called Solomon, an antique dealer who has the contract to supply and curate the Corinthia's upcoming renovation. Needless to say he's eager to retain this project and was willing to lend a hand in understanding the identity of the bottle's anonymous seller. He texted me saying he'd visited the front desk and left a note for me but couldn't stick around as he was extraordinarily busy. The truth was Solomon felt sullied by our little transaction and didn't want to have to physically hand me whatever nugget he'd snouted from the annals of London's antiquities underworld.

I set off to the front desk from the penthouse, the 1950s-style cage lift that sinks through the spiral staircase giving my impatience momentary respite as it evoked memories of the Parisian scenes from Cary Grant's *Charade*.

On arrival I adopted the most casual demeanour I could muster and asked Jinhee, the receptionist if there were any messages. She was on the phone but as I went to repeat myself, she spun in her chair and extended her arm to me while still clutching the phone to her ear. In her hand was a small white envelope sealed with the wax mark which only an antique dealer would use, and I tingled with the feeling that I was Hercule Poirot in *Death on the Nile*.

I whipped it from her, tucked it in my right jacket pocket and pretended to study a staff rota. After sufficient time had passed I slipped into the back office and peeled the envelope's lid from the wax. Inside a scrap of paper was folded in two. Snatching it open I read Solomon's spidery writing:

> *Miss. I. Drummond.*
> *Works the Sleeper.*

I opened my phone and typed the name into Google, hungrily searching through all of the I. Drummonds in the UK. Shop assistants, insurance workers, lawyers, designers.

My eyes scanned the relentlessly scrolling pages.

"Imogen Drummond, speech therapist in Stockport, Greater Manchester."

"Ian Drummond, Express Auto in Alnwick, near

Newcastle."

"Iona Drummond, Thatching in Cambridgeshire."

My index finger continued to scroll aggressively.

"Iris Drummond, marketing executive, Poundbury, Dorchester."

"Ivan Drummond Cheese & Wine, St Ives, Cornwall."

Then something that caught my eye like a fish hook in a Hebridean mackerel.

A Facebook page. Isla D – no location. After clicking the link I found it to require friendship with the owner before you could view its content. All that was available for public viewing were the fan pages of which this woman Isla D was a member. From the looks of it she liked Celtic art and disliked birdwatchers or maybe just birds, I couldn't tell. She seemed to enjoy sketching and harboured clear hero worship for the emergency services.

The last fan page listed was the Rail Workers Union.

CHAPTER 29

Darkening Highlands

My mind paints an aerial establishing shot above the train as we move into Scotland, the Scotland that people see on postcards and in movies, the Highlands. It's stunning and I'm struck with a slight pang of regret that I left such a gorgeous country all those years ago. My guilt turns to latent resentment that the Protection Programme cleansed me of my heritage. I feel like there's nothing of this land left in me.

The night is pitch black. I'm purposefully leaving all of the lights in my cabin off to watch the dark mountains emerge through the window.

The folkish flute and string music of *The Wicker Man* plays as the rolling grass folds into grey slate and up into domineering mountainsides.

Entering the highland mountains is like sliding over the tongue and down the throat of some oceanic predator; they engulf your existence and drag you somewhere that regular folk cannot see.

A faint giggle, somewhere outside in the corridor. I lunge and whip the door open but no one is there. I step out and turn right, heading against the train's motion, steadying myself on the walls, scanning for any sounds other than the high-pitched white noise of the train in the darkness. There is a small refreshments stall in the far corner of the carriage, closed for the evening, but music is playing from its tiny speaker. Dramatic, orchestral music, long oboe sounds then the jolt of dancing violins. I step closer. I see the crown of a small head beneath the countertop, a child perhaps? My pace quickens slightly but then freezes as I see Isla, but she's tiny, she's shrunken. What on earth is going on? I feel nauseous and the taste of flint once again visits the back of my mouth and my nostrils. I feel vulnerable but excited.

CHAPTER 30

A Frozen Cell

I'm walking down the train. I don't know which carriage and I'm not sure how I got here. I look down at my watch to orient myself and am further perplexed to see my Teenage Mutant Ninja Turtles watch that I wore as a boy, where my Omega should be. The train layout maps are gone from the corridor walls, as are the navigation signs.

The carriage must be under renovation, I think to myself, and start walking towards the door into the next one, a little unsteady on my feet.

On opening the door I'm met by the same black corridor and bare walls. I turn around sharply, looking behind to try and make sense of it. I start to walk again, this time more briskly, bracing myself with my hands on each wall as I do.

I throw open the door to the next carriage; it's the same, it's like a mirror or something. There's nothing there, no lights, no cabins, no signs, it's as though the train suddenly became derelict. I'm picking up pace now, I'm into a jog, the exercise tracker on my wrist says my heart rate is actually failing to levels beyond calm, which frightens me more. My pace quickens. I'm into a full sprint, crashing through carriage doors which seem to come every five feet instead of every seventy-five. Bang! Bang! Over and over. Glancing out of the window I see the beginning of the lowlands, green marshes, a huge ancient pine tree and gloomy night skies; they're frozen still. Each window is like the same frame from a movie reel. I'm thrashing through carriage upon carriage now and the train wheels are chattering, the engine is roaring. This cannot be! I'm running at full speed, crashing through carriages with the train travelling at hundreds of miles per hour but the scene outside doesn't move, it's the same marsh, the same pine, even Hitchcock's birds in the sky don't flap their wings, in suspended animation. The feeling of such speed in a world frozen in time makes me nauseous and as I'm about to collapse in exhaustion, I crash through a final door and realise I'm back in my cabin. The train is rocking its calm, consistent cradle, the marshes sweep by outside and overhead there are small lampshades blinking.

CHAPTER 31

A Familiar Stranger

The sun is rising now and we're twenty minutes from our destination, Fort William. I can feel the train engines gradually and almost imperceptibly slowing, downshifting through the gears, applying more resistance to the rails in preparation. Rustling and cupboard clicks can be heard through the walls as my neighbours pack their things and ready themselves to disembark. As I sit quietly in my cabin I hear the clink of glass bottles on a trolley and Isla slows at my door and peers around the frame, sheepishly clutching her clipboard.

"We're nearly there, my lovely. It's been wonderful to have you on board and we do hope to see you again soon."

I stare back at her, studying her cheeks, her eyebrows, her jawline, straining to see my childhood friend beneath her years. She's there;

under the three decades of anguish and sorrow, my friend Sorrell's face is staring back at me.

My eyes flit down rapidly to the scribbles on her clipboard and the realisation hits me, that the character sketched all over the paper is her little brother Jack. An imperceptible smile creeps across my face.

I want to shout "Sorrell, it's me! I've missed you! Like when Tom Hanks sees his wife again after years of being stranded on the island in *Cast Away*."

I want to bellow, "Where have you been these past thirty years? Have you struggled as much as I have? Do you still think about Castlebay?"

But I don't.

"Thanks very much, Isla. You've made the journey worth it."

I notice the exercise tracker on my wrist is showing 41 beats per minute. I am beyond calm.

CHAPTER 32

Birds of a Feather Flock Together

Whenever a new Sanderling joined the class, their first step was a friendly initiation: to draw themselves using finger paints and adorn their self-portrait with actual sanderling feathers.

That morning I waited until Mum had to leave for one of the many calls she'd receive as our minute school's simultaneous teacher, bursar, headmistress and receptionist and I reached for the old piece of my father's fishing rope that Mum had decorated the south side wall of the classroom with, something she used as an aid for when Sanderlings learned of Castlebay's fishing history.

"Now's our chance!" I whispered.

"Positions everybody!" exclaimed Simone.

Everyone rushed to their Sanderling self-portrait and plucked the feathers from the dried glue holding them to the thick, rippled art paper.

I ran to the heavy, solid wooden door of the classroom to peer through the window which was set halfway up and just about my eye level. I scanned the corridor and saw Mum jog purposefully into our tiny assembly hall.

I turned to see Kerin clambering to be first up onto her stool, her competitiveness as strong as ever. In her haste to position her stool next to the bookcase she had failed to see that her classmates were not at the same stage of progression in their preparations. Simone had just finished fixing her feathers in a hurried and haphazard manner and was kneeling between Jack and Bobo, almost shaking with the excitement of flying for Miss Rhona. Jack and Bobo looked suddenly lost, like an infantile sixth sense was telling them this would not go as planned, that danger was imminent.

I recall not an excitement but an impatience. I wanted it done. I'd waited long enough. I'd had to watch as each one of these horrid little creatures fed off my mother like she was some sort of sow. Jack with his relentless, needy arms stretching out to her for reassurance. Bobo's inane chatter that my mother would have to stoop to, tilting her head towards the little cretin, having to feign interest. Simone pushed Mum to breaking point with her constant wanderings, that moronic, detached brain that could not hold focus for longer than three seconds before a speck of dust had snatched her attention and disrupted everyone around her. And Kerin, whose "ambition was far beyond her years", whose "hunger for any kind of learning" left Mum scrambling to create new learning material for her.

Each one of them was utterly oblivious to the fact that they had taken my mother's focus off that which she should have focused on most.

I had registered that Sorrell was absent but the desire to complete my plan took over. It was today. I'd waited long enough.

Now each of them was utterly oblivious to the fact that they were readying their own suicides.

I can picture myself now, walking calmly back toward them, their leader, a general inspecting his dithering troops. It would be done soon.

"Wait, did you see!?" I exclaimed.

The four Sanderlings turned sharply in unison from their respective positions to enquire.

"What!?" Bobo said, clearly a little startled.

"Off your feathers, you mustn't have seen it, but you surely felt it!?"

"What, what?" pleaded Jack, increasingly unnerved.

"The sparkles that just fell from your sanderling feathers, Bobo…"

"What!? She beamed.

"Yes, I knew it, I knew the feathers were still magic, even though they've been stuck on our paintings all this time."

"There! You too, Jack." His face shone with pride as he wiggled his torso to try and catch a look at my fabrication.

This all had the desired effect on Kerin's hideous one-upmanship and Simone's pathetic mind. "What about us!?"

"We'll keep watching, maybe it's different if you're a bit older like we are." This seemed to satisfy Kerin somewhat while Simone was clearly content and went back to feverishly dressing her flying costume with dirty little trinkets she'd brought in from home.

I scampered over to my painting and took a second to assess my classmates' abilities. Mine was clearly the worst. The colours. The shapes. All of it. Even though it was the only one to still have its feathers, next to the others it was still the lesser quality. My stomach grew hot and I ripped four feathers from my painting.

"Wait up, I'm coming," I shouted, pinning my last feather to my shoulder.

"You're doing it wrong," Kerin uttered in a slow, patronising tone.

My stomach grew hotter still. I ran to the door to peer through the window once more. "OK, I think she's nearly here."

"Can you see her!?" Simone brimmed excitedly, her face now almost the same shade of fiery red as her hair.

Kerin finished helping Jack make the final step onto the top of the bookcase. It was all set. Simone stood knees bent, bouncing with adrenaline on the far left. Bobo stood on her left-hand side, staring up at her, trying to process this strange emotion erupting from Simone; her chattering had ceased for a while now. Kerin was next in line, still preening herself, looking like an image-conscious Olympic diver, positioning her toes on the edge of the bookcase with military precision. Jack stood to her left, his tiny fist grippinf the waistband of her green frilly skirt, confusion and uncertainty painted on his face.

And there it was. My real painting. My real colours. "Leave space for me, Simone," I whispered with urgency.

"Kerin, pull down the flying loops... everyone, heads in arms out!" We'll fly like real sanderlings for Miss Kinkade."

The wall behind my four classmates grew clearer. I could see the moulded patterns in the wallpaper, I could see the knots in the wood of the bookcase, the bobbles on Kerin's cardigan; I felt almost complete.

Simone, Bobo and Kerin stood with their chins resting on the thick, salty old sea rope, but Jack was stepping backwards. "KERIN!" I barked and all four started with surprise. I was losing concentration for the first time. "Can you help Jack, he can't be the only one left out while we all fly for Miss Rhona."

Kerin followed my instruction and lifted him through the rope, his face becoming petrified, his sky blue pullover caught on stiff strands of the frayed rope.

"OK, we're a flock, we stick together, stand close and hold hands."

I stepped onto Bobo's stool, the first step up the makeshift mountain that the four had constructed to reach the top of the bookcase. The next step was an old crate, another one of Mum's artistic touches to transform the classroom into the harbour. Now the last step was onto an old dresser that stored the various stationery. I shimmied along it and stepped up onto the dusty top of the bookcase.

The tangle of boxes and furniture legs rumbled precariously beneath me as I climbed.

I summited the mountain of wood and cardboard and joined my victims. They stared back at me over their shoulders, collectively, as one, looking for leadership, Kerin and Simone wrapping the two smaller classmates in almost maternal arms.

I stepped forward, no longer able to mask my intentions with jovial instruction or fake excitement. Kerin was my only equal in terms of physical size and so my instincts took me to her.

"Will we, will it wor—" she muttered as I looped the chunky rope around her neck.

I didn't answer.

The rest looked at me. The classroom was still.

With each hand I wrapped an extra loop around Simone, Bobo and then Jack, snot now streaming from his nose through his anxiety.

I looked out over the classroom, across the room where I'd watched them steal from me each school day, thieving my mother from me right before my eyes.

"No, no, no!" Kerin cried out, finally suppressing

her desire to achieve at challenges and listening to the primal alarm within her spine telling her this was all very, very wrong. I eased my weight through her back. "NO!" she screamed.

SNAP!

Creak.

It was done. Her weight pulled the rest of the line tight.

They swung together, a tangled mess of birds caught in a line. Slowly swinging in a circular motion. Birds of a feather flock together. They'd all inflicted such pain on me, this was only right.

As in life, Simone was the most kinetic of the group, spluttering and twitching for the seconds it took me to descend the chair and box mountain.

By the time I was back on the ground, there were only sporadic flinches from the blue faces.

I suddenly felt a sharp stab of loneliness and the magnitude of the image before me began to wrap its talons around me. A taste emerged in my mouth. The same that arrived whenever I had been struck in the head while play-fighting or clumsily bumped it on a long worktop in The Craigard. A strong, bitter taste that travelled from the top of the back of my skull and slithered about my tongue.

In the haze of emotions I realised the tableau was incomplete, justice was still not fully mine. Sorrell was not swinging. Sorrell had perhaps been the biggest culprit of all. Having my mum come out to give her private tutoring. Unbridled focus while I entertained myself outside sitting in that old rowing boat in their garden. She should be hanging too, I scowled to myself.

I walked over to my mum's desk and slid open the shallow, old, warped oak drawer. My hands moved with purpose as the bric-a-brac of her life tumbled through my small slender fingers. It reminded me of my desperate search on Boyd's houseboat, only this time I knew what I was looking for.

And there it was, the rusted old gold Yale lock key with the Fraserburgh keyring.

I strode back across the centre of the room, past the swinging bodies that were already emitting curious odours. I heaved the heavy door open by leaning my weight backwards and clinging onto the door handle. I stepped through, conducted the same action in reverse until the door was almost closed, at which point I turned the handle and gently slid it into its sturdy frame, releasing the handle in my hand and checking over both shoulders.

My hand slipped the heavy gold key into the lock chamber and rotated it until I heard a clunk.

I placed the key at my feet, and gave it a soft nudge with my trainered toe, so that it shot under the door and finished by the rug at the centre of the room.

I turned and walked casually towards the toilet. I moved along the lino floor lined with grip dots and turned right at the coat hooks which run perpendicular to the walkway. I peered through the coats to check that the teaching assistant, who also doubled as receptionist and cleaner, was sitting at her desk near the front door with her back to me. She was.

I crept through the coats and opened the boys' toilets before stepping inside. The cocoon of the tiled toilets gave me some brief security. I tried to pass urine for effect but couldn't. I stepped over to the basins and looked into the mirror; to my surprise I was smiling broadly. I paused for a moment, looking at the clown-like face staring back at me, vacant.

Time for the final step. Miss Monroe had not found her soul's profession. Her job did not stimulate her and so whenever one of the Sanderlings would walk past her desk she would pounce in desperation for conversation, even from six-year-olds.

As I exited the toilets I let the door slip into the frame, put my hands in my pockets and caught my reflection in the front window to rearrange my features to something more normal.

With my feathers still attached, I walked into the corridor behind her desk, sat down on the end of the bench, hung my head and began gently swinging my feet so that my heels would knock against the wood panel and produce a low thud.

Miss Monroe's head rose slightly from her paperwork, which was almost certainly actually a sketch of the flowers on her desk. My left heel caught the wood again and with it her head rose like a startled Labrador.

With the third thud she turned around. "Clay, hello little sausage."

"Hmmm," I answered, still staring at my battered old white trainers.

"Oh dear that does not sound good, has Mumm–sorry," she corrected herself, "Miss Rhona sent you out of class?"

"Nooo," I exclaimed with rising, immature intonation.

"Then what is it, sausage?"

"Well I'm not a flying Sanderling, that's for sure."

"What?" Miss Monroe replied with a bubble of laughter that said she found my response endearingly cute.

"They're all flying, they said they are the flock and I'm not in the flock because I'm the teacher's kid."

"That's not very nice, is it" she said, with a tone that people use for the elderly or non-English speakers.

I shook my head in silence and heard her heart break.

"Well, why don't you come with me?" she said, getting out of her seat and striding towards me with an outstretched hand. She wore peach-coloured light materials that flowed when she walked.

"And let's get you back with your flock; see, you even have your feathers on, little Sanderling."

The train is panting slowly as we draw alongside

Fort William station platform. I feel as though I've been on this train a lifetime. It really is a unique experience. The advert says it transports you back in time and it certainly delivered on that for me.

As I pack up my toiletries, book, sanderling feather and clothes Keyser Söze leans into my ear and whispers, "The greatest trick the devil ever pulled was convincing the world he didn't exist."

CHAPTER 33

Fort William

It's 08:30 and we have arrived. Fort William. The final stop, the final destination, and the platform is heaving with people. Light is bursting through the cloud and we trudge together as one breathing fog of condensation.

As I walk my eyes scan for her, for Sorrell. I enjoyed our little chats throughout the journey. After a minute or so I finally see her checking her bum bag clips and zipping up her Caledonian Sleeper waterproof coat. She walks right by me but I continue to face forward so she doesn't see me.

For all the lovely things we discussed when she was fetching refreshments and changing the bins, there was one thing we did not cover; that on 7th January in 1991 she caught a winter cold, causing her to stay at home in bed instead of heading into Castlebay Primary to celebrate the culmination of her brother Jack's first year at school. By mid-morning her village had become the scene of a horrific incident, of Scotland's Darkest Day, and she'd lost her little brother. Her family had immediately moved to the mainland to escape the pain of losing their son in the unspeakable event. And in doing so I'd lost track of her. But now, thirty years later, I've found her; I've found where she studied, where she holidayed and now, as a grown woman saddled with emotional scars and anxiety, where she works: on board the Caledonian Sleeper train, a journey which takes her far from the pain of Scotland every day, but returns her to her family the next morning. They never had been able to be away from each other since Classroom B.

CHAPTER 34

Closure

I hear some movement which sounds as if it is inside the building and for a second I think it's going to start early. I hold my breath and force the build-up of inner chest pressure to my ears in a strange attempt to make them capture more sound. But there's nothing.

Only a few hours ago I followed Sorrell off the train platform, into the Nevis Corner Shop and Chemist, and stood in the greetings card section. She was discussing the delivery of her father's depression prescription to her home. It's fascinating how much private information people will divulge in a completely public setting when it's regarding the delivery of something they've purchased. Obliviously and publicly, she stated that she had other errands to run but would be home from mid-morning, "Around 10:45, Wallace Drive, number 33, thanks." She was over an hour late. I know this because I have been sitting in her bedroom since 09:00.

She arrived home at almost 12:00 clearly having underestimated the amount of time these errands would require. I imagine she was laden down with assorted groceries and bags because the door swung open and bounced against the wall as if having been awkwardly nudged with a knee.

I heard her move between the living room, kitchen and study with haste, and clanging doors were a common sound for the first twenty minutes as she stocked the fridge and retrieved nondescript items from what I assumed from the sound was a bureau.

At sporadic points in the morning Sorrell climbed her open-plan stairs. Initially this movement was difficult to hear due to the wonderfully soft and foamy cream-coloured carpet underfoot. This had clearly been laid recently as it was immaculate throughout and still cushioned your feet with every step. The benefit of being positioned in this wardrobe for just over three hours is that my hearing has adjusted to a more heightened level, allowing me to sense where Sorrell is in the house and map her potential next steps.

Around fifteen minutes ago her frenzied scurries subsided and after hearing the click signalling that the kettle had boiled the noises she was making became less frequent, so she was most likely enjoying a cup of the Chelsea green tea I'd noticed on the kitchen worktop on my way in. I reached for my phone to check its switched off and cannot be tracked.

What happened next was utterly perfect. Sorrell's mobile phone rang and she answered it, activating the speakerphone setting, probably to allow her to continue pruning and rearranging her home, as the voice on the phone gently uttered, "Hello my love, are you OK?"

Very few people in the world pitch this question as the opening to a phone conversation, the affection so potent in those six words that it was obvious who the caller was. "Ah hey, Mumma, yeah, I'm better today."

Given my fascination with human detail, idiosyncrasies, the "good stuff", what followed gave me huge pleasure. It was a torrent of raw, honest and personal information discussed between two people who held the closest bond known to mankind: mother and child.

This is Sorrell. Sorrell likes being in the smallest room of her house when it's raining and dislikes seabirds as their feathers remind her of her family's first home in Castlebay on the Hebridean island of Barra.

Sorrell likes raising money for her local emergency services and dislikes the prominence of social media in the lives of her friends.

Sorrell likes a man at work named Cameron, telling her friends it's because he is well-read and bilingual when it's actually because he resembles Kevin of '90s band Backstreet Boys and reminds her of the electricity of finding her sexuality.

Sorrell worries that her father Eric has still not moved on from the loss of her little brother Jack thirty years ago but she likes that her sketches of him bring Eric joy.

Sorrell feels defined by a brush with death at age ten and so is struggling with the idea of having children despite her mother's daily cajoling.

At eight o'clock my newfound super hearing told me that the tired pats across the carpet meant Sorrell was heading towards her bedroom. The wardrobe is not a walk-in but is larger than average. It is around ten feet wide and four feet deep with white concertinaed doors made from lightweight wood. It houses Sorrell's extensive summer garments, cramped together, all hanging from the sagging gold bar overhead. The space also doubles as storage for what I can only assume are Eric's old naval uniforms.

On entering the wardrobe just after nine, I positioned myself behind two large, green storage sacks that were in good condition but had clearly not been moved for months, located on the left-hand side of the floor space if one is looking outward.

Starving myself of visual stimulation, my sole sight for the last three hours has been through a slit, the fractional space between the body of a silk, beige trench coat and the right sleeve which hangs beside it. My world since 09:05 has been darkness punctured by this slit of light.

I watch Sorrell move about her bedroom; the intimacy between my unaware partner and me is palpable. What strikes me most is how she is able to operate in silence for large portions of time: no TV, no radio, no podcast, no music. I've become an expert in the sounds of her still house. Its clicks, rolls and clunks constantly paint visual pictures for me as I mentally follow Sorrell around her feminine room. She conducts a form of nightly routine but is often distracted. While checking her mobile phone voicemails her autopilot gaze slides to her foot where she notices an imperfection on her skin, which she proceeds to inspect with the concentration of a neurosurgeon.

She removes her jeans, staggering over to the wardrobe and reaching with an outstretched arm to steady herself as she peels them down past her shins and I catch the intimate, feminine smell of sweat mixed with day-old moisturiser and perfume.

A myriad of fragrances penetrate the wardrobe door slats and fill my grateful nostrils. Vanilla, tea tree oil and the clinical smell of make-up cleanser waft inward, illustrating the regimented routine of Sorrell's bedtime.

Sorrell twice opens the wardrobe and my face is mercifully gifted with a wave of fresh air. A glance at my fitness tracker shows my heart rate had soared an entire two beats per minute higher than the coma level it had dropped to throughout my wait: 42 bpm is indicative of your grandma's heart rate just after her afternoon chamomile and just before she drops off to sleep.

I watch Sorrell climb into bed and settle and I clutch the toy train that had been stored in a corner of the closet. The sheets float down and rest against the curve of her legs and torso and she exhales a breath. The breath was one of tiredness, even exhaustion, but also of satisfaction, an exhalation that said: "My god, life is throwing all sorts at me but I'm coping, I'm surviving, I'm doing pretty well."

As I watch Sorrell stare at the ceiling in the dim light of her bedside lamp, I sense she is doing that thing we all do, where we mentally run through life and gradually down-change the gears until our eyelids become like anvils and we drift off.

It is only when that final light clicks off and the room plunges into pitch darkness that the enormity of the situation lands.

A sense of pending completeness washes over me. That day in 1991, I had weaponised Kerin's pathetic eagerness to achieve. I had weaponised Simone's utterly moronic energy. I had weaponised Bobo's blind, naive soul-searching and finally I had weaponised Jack's simple, childish excitement. I had convinced them all to take part in my game, climbing up to the beams set in the ceiling of the old school house and persuading them all to enter the noose loops that I had formed. I hung them all, but chance had saved Sorrell.

Just as my hearing had done, my eyes now adapt to the new, drastically different levels of light, which is limited to the drip of moonlight seeping through the curtains. The lack of sight is somehow deafening.

Despite the darkness I can still make out the hazy view of her chest gently rising and falling with deep and long breaths, sleeping soundly. I watch and savour it. While saliva drools from my gaping mouth, I silently open the wardrobe door and, arching on my fingers and toes, creep towards her.

CHAPTER 35

Never Far

There is a darkness in my life which both follows me and guides me. I do feel. I feel upset, I feel rage, I feel delight. But above all I feel a low, humming, hunger to inflict damage on those I meet. There is no correlation between the level of crime I deem you to have committed and the severity of horror I bring to your door. I simply follow the darkness.

There was the barmaid in Glen Coe whose marriage I destroyed.
There was the Dundee bus passenger whose face I maimed.
There was the Glaswegian man buying sex who I burned.
There was the Lake District holidaymaker who I drowned.
There was the Yorkshire office worker whose

family business I ruined.

There was the fellow night student in Bath who still calls me, pleading to get back together.

There were at least two patients at the Royal London who arrived at the wrong floor on their way to emergency theatre.

There was the illegal immigrant cleaner at my Farringdon office whose family I've extorted for three years.

There was the obnoxious restaurant customer who ate black mould in his expensive dinner.

There was the French maître d' who took my job so I took his father's sanity.

There have been numerous Corinthia customers whose financial details I've stolen and sold.

But starting it all, there was Classroom B of Castlebay. Sorrell, Kerin, Simone, Bobo and Jack, who stole my mother's love for me. Sorrell simply postponed the righteous repercussions through ignorant luck.

I remember my Uncle Gordon's friend, the island doctor Fergal Douglas, conducting various tests on me in the weeks that followed Classroom B. Research in later life has shown this to be the Hare Psychopathy Checklist, devised by Canadian psychologist Robert Hare; it evaluates individuals for psychopathic traits. I have since tested myself, studying the traits to monitor any similarities with myself...

Grandiose sense of self-worth.
Sexual promiscuity.
Criminal diversity.
Lack of remorse.
Lack of realistic long-term goals.
Overly impulsive.
Glib affect.
Manipulative behaviour.
Juvenile delinquency.
Lack of empathy.
Pathological lying.

I suppose you could say Dr Douglas's instincts were right, although I remember stealing a look at his notes while he was engrossed in a chess game with my uncle one night. Anyone scoring over 30 is considered psychopathic, meaning my result of 24 or 25 (I can't quite recall which it was) places me in the realms of normality. This means most clinicians would argue that I am towards the larger point on the bell curve of the UK population, more like the general public, a prole if you will. I'm no Michael Myers. I'm no Pennywise the Clown.

But how? I hear you ask. When I am capable of such unspeakable things? Well, maybe the UK experiences darkness every day, maybe psychopathy isn't reserved for the characters of movies or the CEOs of the City. Maybe you can have a job, a partner, a best mate, plans and dreams but still be capable of the most abhorrent actions.

Maybe Wells's time machine novel was more fact than fiction, maybe society is Morlocks eating Eloi. Maybe Hitchcock's Bruno Anthony was right when he said that "my theory is that everyone is a potential murderer".

Maybe there are more of us, hiding beneath the surface. Hiding in the shadow of that bell curve.

Maybe you're never far from one of us.

EPILOGUE

BBC news report

The body of forty-year-old Isla Drummond was discovered earlier this morning at her home address of Wallace Drive, Fort William Scotland.
All details of the case thus far have been withheld from the media; the only details we have come from the Lochaber Police Watch Commander who confirmed Miss Drummond's family have been contacted and her death is being treated as a homicide.

Lochaber Police Report

Fort William Constabulary
Officer: Roy Skelton
Rank: Detective Inspector
Date & Time: 29th July 2021 [21:20]
Crime Ref: 03811AR
Victim: Isla Drummond a.k.a Sorrell Hutch
Description: Coroner reports cause of death was decapitation with a blunt blade or instrument. Attack likely took around 7 minutes from

initiation to death.

Missing fingernails on the left fourth and right third phalanx are considered defensive wounds and were lost during a clawing action in attempts to stop the attack.

Forensic reports state the large volumes of spatter found in the bedroom indicate this as the scene of the homicide. The head of the victim was subsequently moved to the kitchen where it was discovered by first responder Constable F. Sykes.

Initial forensic report finds only Miss Whitwell's DNA in the flat. Feathers on the victims head suggests local wildlife caught the body's scent in the hours before discovery of body by neighbour.

Further action: no current leads at this time.

ACKNOWLEDGEMENT

Jennifer, this novel was my candle and you cupped your hands around the flame, ensuring it never burned out.

The author would like to thank;

Aruna Vasudevan
Lauren Brookes
William Maynard
Ian Howe

Their respective guidance and opinion was pivotal in the creation of this book.

* * *

Printed in Poland
by Amazon Fulfillment
Poland Sp. z o.o., Wrocław

35164313R00099